D1170546

PRAISE *for*

FARMER'S ALMANAC

"These moody, compelling stories about Odette County, Wisconsin, bring to mind other fictional American places, such as Yoknapatawpha County, Spoon River, Gopher Prairie, Port William, and Winesburg, Ohio. Like his predecessors, from William Faulkner to Wendell Berry, Chris Fink shows us characters living on back roads and in small towns with as much drama and dignity, as much passion and perplexity, as one might find in the lives of people anywhere."

—Scott Russell Sanders, author of *Earth Works: Selected Essays*

"Rock-picking, fight-picking, finger-licking, this is muscular writing from deep within the American heartland. *Farmer's Almanac* is full of unexpected tenderness when you were expecting brutality, and ready with all kinds of ructions whenever you think there might be routines. Chris Fink is the authentic voice of American agricultural labour. Watch out, latte-slurping salonnières, he's coming down the river and raising hell!"

—Giles Foden, author of *The Last King of Scotland*

Copyright © 2013 by Chris Fink
All rights reserved
First Edition

For information about permissions to reproduce selections from this book, or to order bulk purchases, write to Emergency Press at info@emergencypress.org.

Book design by Kelly Hobkirk
Illustrations by Brandon Chappell

Fink, Chris
ISBN 978-0-9836932-7-7
1. Fiction—Literary. 2. Fiction—General.

Emergency Press
154 W. 27th St.
#5W
New York NY 10001
emergencypress.org

9 8 7 6 5 4 3 2 1
First printing

Printed in the United States of America
Distributed by Publishers Group West

CHRIS FINK

FARMER'S ALMANAC

A WORK OF FICTION

Emergency Press
New York

TABLE OF CONTENTS

Local Color

Long Range Forecast

About Town

Animal Husbandry

Hunting & Trapping

Heavy Machinery

TABLE OF CONTENTS

Bird Watching

Home & Garden

For My Family

Why doesn't something happen? Why am I left here alone?

— Sherwood Anderson, *Winesburg, Ohio*

You could ask the smartweed; maybe the smartweed knows why.

— Greg Brown, "Walking the Beans"

Local Color

For every man of sense and candour, who reads in order to reap the benefit of reading, will give merit its due, whenever he finds it, and be cautious how he commends. When I meet with a great many beauties in a piece, I am not offended by a few faults. Sometimes too, what is very clear in a book, seems to us obscure, for want of reading it with sufficient attention.

—*The Farmer's Almanac,* 1801

The Bergamot Weekly Almanac

June 17, 2005

SESQUICENTENNIAL EDITION

Slack Lines:
Fetters Sings Swan Song. Says So Long, Bergamot Pond

BY FRANK FETTERS
The Bergamot Weekly Almanac

Bergamot Pond was never blue. For a long time it was actually rather murky. It was full of carp in those days and the scaly bottom-feeders kept the water stirred with their constant foraging of the muddy bottom, an aquatic version of a pig's rooting for food amidst its own feces. If you live in Bergamot Pond environs, as most of you readers do, this analogy should seem appropriate, considering the origins of the lake. The two hundred acres of brownish water was once a hog farm. In the first decade of the 20th century, Claude Bergamot flooded his farm to create the lake. He settled on naming it Bergamot Pond purely for the euphony of the moniker. Bergamot was a pig farmer with a poet's ear.

A dam was built to control runoff, fingerling game fish were stocked and cabins began to appear where farrowing crates had been. Real estate advertisements at the time touted the aquamarine waters of Bergamot Pond. Claude's farm became a vacation destination. But in the 40s came the carp: Bergamot Pond's own blitzkrieg. Many residents here at this time believed the lake was in fact still a farm for swine, only the finned variety. I personally believe the swine of this place have always been legged.

I must confess that I have had a long and sordid love affair with this pond, this pseudo-lake. You all know my eccentricity, my keening for local yore and tendency to dramatize. You see my face and words yellowing in newsprint on tag boards about town. You add coned hats and asses ears. You know me as the editor of this *Bergamot Almanac*, the man whose weeklies are prone to ponder over the character of town founder Pere Bergamot, French Voyageur who spawned the pig farmer who spawned this lake, this town, this existence. I am a redundant fixture here. But on this, the sesquicentennial celebration of our town, our 150th summer, I endeavor to be different. I hazard to turn my lens inward, to give you the intersection of one man and one place. This is to be an unwrapping, the taking out of a long-newspapered ornament.

Because I myself wonder that I came to love this lake lacking in mystery, purity and big fish—those entities for which most lakes are loved. Except that I was farrowed here. Like a Vichy hog trained to snort out truffles, I grew up rooting these shores and muddy bottoms for things that crawled or swam. These things I felt a kinship with. These things I still feel akin to and those with mud as their essence. There are always those who would dredge a mud lake. They don't understand there is no rock or clarity in its nature. Mud returns, fortified.

There are those who cringe at the thought of sinking their bodies into murky water, their feet into muddy bottoms. Of late there are those who would attempt to aerify all things stagnant and putrefied. I rollick in swampiness, rejoice in algae and bog. I am descended from bottom feeders. I am of the breed that crawled forth from the brine on the white skin of our underbellies. I erect no pickets around the outhouse of my soul.

I suppose we don't have much choice where we take root. Bloom where you're planted, my old father used to say. I would not have chosen for myself this place, seemingly barren of cultural fodder. I have had scant occasion to write of wars, national trends, or social movements—these events swirled around this lake, but we were left as a vacuum, unscathed. Neither have there been adulteries, crimes of passion, scant big-fish stories. Nothing remarkable has ever happened here; you people saw to that. As you know I have spent my time writing about your news: your sidewalk and roadwork vetoes, your ongoing battle against municipal sewer, a water tower. Your curfews, boating regulations, fish (ha) limits. Your weddings, obits, weather reports and police blotters. But these Saturdays, in this Op/Ed page, in this space I call *Slack Lines*— this has been the place for my news. My stories have been histories and I have aged here like a history. (You line your bird cages with these, my life's droppings. This double truck should last you.)

But my peculiar roots once prospered in this loamy ground just the same. In my childhood they took well to the sediment-rich soil here and spread unhindered as a vast and pulsing network of capillaries. Then, on a summer's morning, they died. But the brittle remains of this ductwork still extend to caress the bare feet of Bergamot summertime.

In those hay days of the carp epidemic—this would have been forty-odd years after Claude Bergamot, grandson of the

Voyageur, dug a hole and flooded his pig farm—in those days did I begin my boyhood here on Bergamot Pond. In those days was I alive and part of the happenings of this place, not merely a recorder of them. I was the news. I was as you are. Now, in my familiar role as recorder, I recount a specific event that we may garner the universal. I keep my cynical comments to myself when I can help it (though at times I succumb to my nature). I employ humor and pathos in a manner not entirely journalistic for this my farewell address. My celebratory unraveling begins, my parting gift to Bergamot Pond.

*   *   *   *   *

In 1955, the population of Bergamot Pond was mostly transient. We would pack up from our various Wisconsin localities and arrive here in late May, in time to drop docks into water, roll back window canvas and beat out mattresses. We fixed on the mundane. We came to Bergamot Pond to avoid outside news. Families normally concerned with national news, work and school, focused instead on preservation of our very heart, our Bergamot Pond. All residents turned to Lake President Konrad Huber for the first order of business: the mounting carp concern—responsible for the diminishing of our lake's transparency and the stunting of the game fish population. Huber surmised that the best way to restore a respectable clarity to the water—if not an airy blueness— was to get rid of the carp. A self-proclaimed humanitarian and a windbag of the first rate, Huber didn't favor a whole-sale butchering of the fish, which was possible through conventional poisoning. Rather, he decided to give the fish a fighting chance and in the meantime turn a profit. He would buy them, a sign on the lakefront bulletin by the public landing declared, beginning June 17, Father's Day, for a nickel a carcass. But no one yet knew how he'd recover the money—fish his fortune—as the saying went.

It was already June, and the adult population of Bergamot Pond was abuzz with talk of Huber's strange marketing ploy. I recall the scuttlebutt. Did he wish to eat the fish? Did he have some fangled pickling recipe that would make the gummy and rancid carp flesh flaky and fragrant? Or would he smoke them on tremendous racks along the lake and fumigate all the neighbors? He was a schemer, that flat-pated kraut—did he plan on selling his new recipe for pickle-smoked carp chunks and making a double-profit?

The kids' sector of the lake thought less about Huber's grand-scheme—though we heard enough about it at dinner tables—and more about silvery coins: wheelbarrows full of them. Amidst the grown-up furor over how Huber was going to somehow pollute our beloved lake with his smelted concoctions, there was a parallel and equally fervent movement among the children. That June we mustered into a veritable fish-farming machine with a shared entrepreneurial vision: the accruement of cash via carp carcasses. Within a week of Huber's dramatic posting, the shores and waters of Bergamot Pond were littered with browned bodies, both of dying bottom feeders and of the boys and girls casting, dipping, trolling, jigging, spearing and plunking for them.

On Father's Day Huber would accept the carp on his back doorstep, though most of us kids on the lake had a week's head start on him. He hadn't mentioned, after all, whether he required the carp to be fresh. So, by the eve of opening day, my sister Alberta and I had already snagged 15 of the mud suckers and had them lined up in neat rows by the shoreline for all to see. Passersby would remark about those lousy carp and the way they made the water muddy. They would kick the carp, and I learned an early lesson in species discrimination. You release a game fish or put it immediately out of its misery while you let a carp suffer and die. I looked around Bergamot Pond and made connections. You put a painted turtle in a tank to enjoy it—you hack the head from a snapping turtle to get rid of it. You feed the orioles, buntings, cardinals—pellet the dirty-damned starlings, our immigration mistakes. You persecute the base, the unlovely—you assimilate and praise the beautiful. But the persecuted adapt, fortify, outnumber the pampered beautiful.

Those carp stayed alive for hours there on the lawn because they didn't flop or cavort like a game fish would. They conserved their energies, moving only for occasional gulps of air—yes, they could breathe air—so much out of water. Their soft, bluish lips gasped for it. Alberta and I would step on them barefooted to force their mouths permanently open. Their slime felt cool on the arches of our feet. When we stepped off, they would breathe again. The ugly sometimes adore the lovely. So their adoration kept them alive. They saw blue sky with their one eye upward, and that was enough to make them hold their breath, conserve that panorama. At night they saw our stars and died beneath them.

Yes, I can close my eyes and conjure that summer, opening day arriving with a west wind that swept across Bergamot Pond's muddy waters, over 15 stiff shoreline carp carcasses, and up the steep hill to our two-roomed, wide-windowed cottage, where it woke most of the dozen or so sleepers therein, all my visiting relatives, to the gamey smell of ripening carp. To Alberta, who was buried in her sleeping bag on the floor, and to me, it was a sweet aroma, our first scent of real money. We wasted no time on good mornings or blueberry flapjacks that day, just slipped into our still-damp swim suits and weaved our way through a houseful of groggy, complaining adults and out the screen door to Bergamot morning.

With the grass still plenty wet from a dewy night, we took our morning dip. Alberta was a fish with feet and nothing could keep her out of the water. As her older brother, I was her keeper, her permanent babysitter. Together we suffered through numerous bouts of swimmer's ear, a product of Bergamot Pond's polluted water.

After our swim, we loaded Pop's shallow wheel barrow with all 15 carp, ranging in length from just over a foot to just under two. They were slippery fish and the top few kept sliding off as I bullied the rusted wheel barrow up the steep hill to our cabin and in the direction of Shore Drive. Smaller, weaker Alberta had the job of scooping the scaly flop-overs while stronger, more important brother pushed the main load. I made sure to keep her scrambling by tilting the wheel barrow unnecessarily a few times, fake-straining from the burden. Unsuspecting Alberta was duly impressed by my prowess and more than happy to do her meager part. This posturing was necessary, I realized even at the tender age of twelve, to keep my ten-year-old sister in check and in awe of her brother.

"Happy Fadder's Day Popalopagus," Alberta said proudly to our dad. He had opened the screen door with a scowl, presumably because the stench had become stronger. As usual, he was bare-chested and bare-footed, therefore as close to a kid as any of the adults on our lake.

"Bless my spectacles," Pop returned, honking his Roman nose into his ever-present red hanky. "Wattaya gonna go and stink up my wheelbarrow with those uglies for?" Pop knew exactly what was going on. He just liked to play dumb, a game between he and Alberta. Pop was an original. Like Alberta, always naming things foreign. He and Alberta had a freedom with language, a special way to talk to each other that always made me feel left out. These pages deserve to be graced with my sister's voice, too long absent from the shores of Bergamot Pond.

"Taking them to President Huber, Doody," Alberta beamed. "Frank's gonna gimme a whole quarter!"

I retorted quickly, "Time to go or we'll be late and Huber'll give away all his shiny nickels already. Move it. Ship out. Bye Pop. Oooga Oooga."

But before I could wheel us away, Pop caught on to my math and sung out after us: "Bring those 15 nickels into the cabin when you get back Frank, and I'll help you two split 'em up, fifty-square. After that you can scrub the stink outta my wheel barrow."

"Bye Poppy," chimed Alberta, that brat. Pop watched us leave the drive, though Alberta didn't know it. He was watching to make sure I kept an eye on my sister. That was my job, Pop said, sometimes with his belt. That was my most important job.

Huber's place was, still is, half a mile around Shore Drive, up Heartbreak Hill, by Dregg's Point and around sundry wooded curves. I could easily have gotten revenge on Alberta in one of those deeply-shaded valleys by telling her how the giant tree toads liked to piss foamy buckets on little girls' heads, leaving them warty and unmarriageable, but truth be known, those carp got damned heavy and I had all I could handle to keep from taking a break and damaging my superhero's status in Alberta's eyes.

When we finally parked our freight in Huber's brightly sunned driveway, it was to the sight of Orville Duncan trundling out of Huber's dark garage with a fat wad of nickels in his pudgy fist. Duncan was about our age, one of the many bounty hunters on our lake: the opposition. We nodded respectfully. We had business to attend.

We trucked our load into Huber's garage, and he came out carrying a canvas money bag and a can of beer. He started in with his trademark verbosity. "Fine specimens, kids," he said. "Truly fine manure. Why that load you have there is perfection personified, magnificence multiplied. *Eine, zwei, drei, vier,* Huber's gonna have a beer." After he took a head count on the deceased, he counted the fifteen coins into my sweaty palms. When I asked Huber what he'd do with the carp, he aimed a droopy arm over to his half-acre B-lot.

"Take 'em over there with the other victims," he said, and I wheeled the carp over to a six-foot pyre of carp-flesh, gave our load the old heave-ho. The carp stunk and crushed each other with their own weight. Their skins dried in the sun and flies ate their eyes. Next to the pile was a giant yellow earth mover Huber must have rented to manage the mound.

I let Alberta scoot the empty wheel barrow home while I fingered the loot. "What's he gonna do with that pile of carp?" she asked.

"Don't be a bother to brother," was my trademark reply. I was too busy doing calculations to worry about it. The way I figured, the money would buy four cans of Green Giant's brightest canned corn. Tomorrow we'd go back to work hauling carp out of Bergamot Pond, cleansing our heart and soul.

By that mid-afternoon, it was clear to those interested that Huber didn't plan to cook the carp, else he wouldn't have let them bloat out there in the sun. There was some talk that he might incinerate them for an alternative energy source. But a consensus was being formed on boat docks, under crabapple trees and against pump houses around the lake that he was going to use them for gardening. Vic Beedle, a radio reporter for WVIK in Shady Valley said there was a University of Wisconsin extension grant on the loose for new ideas in crop fertilization. Last year, Vic's cat dragged a small carp up to his squash patch and there bloomed and burgeoned one of the biggest butternuts he had ever seen. Vic's dollar was on the notion that Huber had wheedled that extension grant.

Next morning, armed with canned corn and fishing rods, Alberta and I rowed Pop's leaky green rowboat out on Bergamot Pond. The carp were thick that morning and many were sucking algae off the glassy surface as I strained against the oars. Every so often I struck a humpback carp with a wooden oar, creating havoc on the smooth surface.

Those early years rowing with my sister up front, I remember how the world of the lake would open up to me. It would open in hindsight, for I faced backwards, yet my forward direction was true. Every stroke of the oars would reveal a new slice of my world to the periphery of either side. Those few of you who know Wordsworth will remember how he rowed similarly on Ullswater while Rydal Head loomed larger and larger over the stern of his boat with every stroke, as if pursuing him. The mountain grew with the distance. As the young poet rowed forward he came to know what was behind him, and by the proximity of past events, where he was going.

So do I wish to hone my aim with this exercise in rowing, of opening up the past. Wordsworth rowed his whole life on his own lake, as I have rowed my whole life on this. I have been persistent, for I have come to believe that, finally, we can row only on our own lake, and when we venture off we are lost. It is only now I remember that Alberta, too, was facing backward in Pop's rowboat. She must also have had the world open up in hindsight, except that in the middle of her aperture was always her brother, rowing. I was her vanishing point. How I wish I could have her back again.

Bergamot Pond indeed has a central spring—that spot where the pig farmer first hit water—and Alberta and I headed for it, to catch our carp. Every lake has a principal source, its Calvinist heart, but the spring on Bergamot Pond is woeful. It is as a songbird's small heart fluttering in the breast of a sow. Nonetheless it was and is the deepest part of Bergamot Pond, and Alberta and I would row there mostly for the mystery of deep water. At that time the spring was said to be thirty feet deep, fathomless for us. And I always knew we were at the spring—though there are no markers—when on my right were the twin weeping willows, their branches drooping waterward in tandem desolation, and on my left was Dregg's Point, site of the old road, the only road, through this slough, and behind me, where I faced, was our tiny cottage, wide windows as eyes to the lake.

And there at the spring Alberta and I fished, for the better part of a month. We lured the carp by spraying the water with corn kernels, and we waited, peering downward over the gunnels, the water sometimes reaching up and touching our noses, we peered so hard. When we saw the yellow kernels blotted out by dark shapes, occasionally reappearing, we knew the frenzy was on, and we'd put lead to line, string our hooks with four or five kernels and cast.

We threw back the occasional stunted game fish and stacked the bottom of that rowboat with heavy carp, day in, day out. In between fish we'd munch on the cold corn and Alberta and I would laugh and make jokes about turning into carp, we ate so much corn. Sometimes she would tangle her line, and I would take her pole from her, feigning anger. I'd fix it with a flurry of showmanship.

Other kids were out on the lake as well. Adults too joined in the fray, as not many wanted to swim in the foul water. Alberta and I became mechanized so that the tugs on our lines registered only as the clinking of coins, and our hearts did not jump when something from fathoms down tugged against us. Sometimes we'd wrestle three-foot behemoths, and we'd happily land these together anticipating Huber's extra change. And we'd rest our bare feet on the pile of carp in Pop's boat. Sometimes Alberta would flop overboard, unable to resist a swim, and I'd pull her in with a flexed forearm when she was ready. Each afternoon we'd row home, and on each trip home I'd let the familiar view from our lakefront guide me home as it opened up behind me. Evenings, shorefronts around the lake would display their elongated catch.

Alberta would inevitably beg for another swim, and sometimes I'd join her in the water and pull her under. When I let her up, she'd squeal with delight. "Do it again. Do it again." Sometimes I'd wait watchful on the pier, the evening scenery darkening.

To this day my favorite pastime is to row on Bergamot Pond. Only now, as you know, there are no carp here. There haven't been for years. But I scarcely need to remind you newer residents, with your improved houses and manicured lakefronts, of Bergamot Pond's new concern: our seaweed epidemic. Now the water is indeed crystalline, yet we can't see it under the dense matting of weeds. The carp are gone and the sun shines brightly through the gin-clear water to spawn the weeds. Now no finned hogs are here to uproot them. Now all of your motor boats sit uselessly on their lifts, and my shoulders and oarlocks strain doubly under the great weight of the weeds on their oars.

I think back to that summer and its end. Our impressive profits wasted buying marked-up corn. Huber surrendered his war with the carp, stuck with two tons of rotted fish flesh after the university extension withdrew further grant money citing more pressing concerns. You could go down to Huber's and load up wheelbarrows of free carp flesh for gardening if you wanted. Bergamot made state news because of our insignificance. I vaguely remember: *Tiny Bergamot Misses Big Break*. We were tossed like small fish back into the murky waters of anonymity.

And then there was the poisoning. Town fathers raided the coffers to poison the carp. The liquid toxin was brought in tanker trucks and pumped into the lake. Within hours, thousands of carp went belly up. The poison: liquid swine slurry pumped from the slurry store at Tabor's Duroc farm. This turned our blessed water into ammonia, suffocating everything alive in Bergamot Pond. More money was needed for carp removal. All private craft were recruited to scoop dead carp from our waters; Alberta and I made a half-dollar an hour with Pop's row boat. We loaded dump trucks at the public landing and these were seen rumbling along Shore Drive for a week. The pavement ruptured, causing further budget woes.

By August, the waters of Bergamot Pond shone crystal clear, but swimming was forbidden. Alberta was disoriented, and I had to spray her down with the garden hose twice a day. A west wind brought a sulfurous odor up the hill to our cottage. By the end of August, weeds had infested the dead lake. A pall was cast over our heart of hearts.

*   *   *   *   *

I offer you this story because most of you weren't alive in 1955, and those of you who were haven't learned your history lessons. You are like the Voyageurs who paddle in their swift canoes, always forward-looking. I have plodded along backwards without claptrap through four carp epidemics, four weed epidemics, as many poisonings, as many lake presidents. Now Walter Hinkle wants to dredge. Says our lake is filling up with muck. Now Herr Hinkle wants to reintroduce a sterile breed of carp that feeds on weeds. People are talking about Walter Hinkle and his scheme. Can you imagine, seeding this water in carp after all the poisoning? The root of the problem remains; we tend to think of our past as pristine. "Let's have our lake clear as it once was," you protest. Let me tell you Bergamot Pond was never blue, and neither was it weedless. Our past is mud, and mud returns, fortified.

By now the motive of my carp narrative should indeed be coming clear, and I will withhold my thesis no longer, for here your news merges with mine. Here I mutter Bergamot Pond's collective, unspoken secret.

Earlier this month, as you know, yet another proposed ordinance requiring municipal sewer was defeated here. You celebrated your saved nickels by toasting neighbors with expensive beer and undercooked bratwursts. When, at dusk, you returned to your improved homes to relieve yourselves, you flushed your liquid and solid waste into rusted and leaking holding tanks. These decrepit antiques overflowed, sending their contents to join the groundwater in a downstream lunge for Bergamot Pond. Like the rest of America, you think that your turds vanish magically when they disappear from your porcelain bowls. They do not. By morning, they were fertilizing the cattails that grow so well at water's edge. In the morning you looked out your bay windows, and what you saw out there was not a lake at all, more a swamp, shallowing annually.

"This is unacceptable," you muttered, "Something needs doing about these damn weeds. Poison maybe." Such has been the litany of our ignorance. For our own excrement has fertilized this lake since its inception. I leave you with this knowledge: a birthday gift to you, a retirement present for myself, an overdue apology to my father, a belated obituary for my sister.

Alberta died in this lake, in the waning days of the summer of 1955—fifty years ago—scant weeks after Huber's poisoning. I found her floating in the water by our pier. I saw a lightly tanned body bobbing in the waves on my way to the dock and thought for a moment that Bergamot Pond's biggest carp had finally gone belly up. Then I remembered the no-swimming ordinance. Then I remembered that Alberta was supposed to be with me that morning. I had told her to go play by herself while I did the important work of changing my bicycle tires. I told her she was getting in the way. A drowning, they called it. My Alberta.

When I turned her over, her eyes were open and her soft bluish lips formed an O. I put my mouth to hers and we exchanged empty breaths.

What happened next is my history. I won't foul these pages. Suffice to say Alberta's Doody boarded up the windows of our cottage, and our family never returned. Gone was his levity of manner, his heart. He boarded up his soul. I returned here as a young man to take this job, to pay my penance. And I am as culpable as you. For fifty years I have wallowed here. And I have toiled as you to get the waters of this pond to come clean.

Country Mile

I used to pick rocks. I worked out on Harlan Worden's acreage picking them one after another. Field stones were the enemy of cultivator sweeps and disc harrows. You couldn't get me to drive the tractor. I just wanted to lift the rocks. It was cheaper for Worden to pay me to pick the rocks than it was to let them lie around and tear up his implements. He paid three an hour straight pay.

Worden must've had a thousand acres and I picked rocks on every one of them. Besides that he rented his crew out and we picked rocks halfway across Odette County. Most people think the corn country is boring, but walking those furrows, I saw how beautiful it all was. That land was alive. Worden said you could plant a penny in that ground on Sunday and harvest a nickel come Monday. It was better ground than there was anywhere. It just took a while to appreciate. You grew up bored with it, wishing it was mountains. You looked at it every day and didn't see anything but rows and rows of rolling nothing. Then one day in October you walked out there and the corn was dry and the shocks were rustling in the wind, and you thought there was no better sound in the world, because in that sound of ripe rustling corn there was life ready to pour out to the world. Silos and silos of it. You realized then, too, that this country had raised you up good and tall, and your roots were so deep and entrenched that you had a better hold on the ground than most anyone you knew.

Fields of corn, wheat, beans and barley and I de-rocked 'em before the crops got too high. I was up at the earliest part of the day to beat the heat of summer. I rode my blue-and-white Schwinn four miles down Hemlock Hollow Road to Worden's farm, holding my sack lunch in my shirt. The crew always met behind Worden's pig barn and the old man came out with the list of fields he wanted us to hit, and then he told us we were burning daylight and went back into his house, back to his toddy, probably. The crew, usually four, sat on the back of the empty hay wagon, and Worden's hired man drove us out to the field in the '59 Johnny Popper—the last of its kind. Our legs dangled off the back of the wagon and we just sat there and looked at our hands and thought about all the work there was to do, even before lunchtime. There was a chill in the air at that hour, about an hour after sunrise, and the four of us sitting there thinking about rocks didn't do much to warm things up.

Pretty soon the wagon would stop, and even if you knew the country pretty well, you'd be at a field that was more like any other field than it was different. You got off the wagon and stowed your lunch in the wheel well of the tractor and the tractor started off down the furrow and you started after it, to pick rocks. Everyone knew his job and it would be a couple of hours before anyone felt like it was time to say anything to anybody. That is, unless there was a new guy that needed breaking in.

There was a trick to know which rocks to pick up and which to leave grow another year. Those guys who could pick rocks could tell the difference. Fist-sized were just small enough to leave. Walking the furrows, watching the rocks, you could spot a fist-sized rock and see that it was too small to bother with because when the disc came by it would just slide off the harrow and lay there harmless as an egg in the turned-up soil. You could actually see that in your head.

Gabe Karp could flat pick. He didn't need a nickname because there were already two in his regular one. Karp was older and had done lots of jobs, including mostly pitching horse shit at Flax Ranch. I'd done that too, winters, so we had lots in common. Except he could fit a whole tin of wintergreen snoose in his front lip and let it drip out so he looked like one of the Elephant Snot Twins. We were different, too, because I was still in high school and Karp and the rest of the crew were done with that forever. And I had an ambition besides picking rocks, which I kept to myself.

Karp had what you needed to have to pick rocks. He had pride in his work. He also knew how to leave the fist-sized rocks lying in the furrow. If you didn't know that you could be finished pretty quick, out with a bad back or shit-canned for being too slow.

Including the foreman, there were five in a crew, if Worden could keep five good men. One drove the old Deere Johnny Popper with the flat hay wagon behind. The rest of us picked rocks. We walked two abreast on each side of the wagon. The inside man, called a center, walked five or six rows away from the tractor. The outside man, the flanker, walked as many as ten rows out from him. Your job was simple. You looked for rocks in the field and you picked them up and threw them on the wagon. All you were looking for in the world was rocks. You tried to work fast so the driver didn't have to stop. If you were a flanker you'd throw your rock into the center, and he'd pick it up and throw it on the wagon for you. Altogether we covered about 40 rows. There ain't a machine outside of Dr. Seuss that'll do that, or for as cheap.

It was lonely work, mostly because of the slow putt-putt-putt the popper made. No one could hear you when you talked to them, so you just shut up. Your feet fell in time with the popper's putt. Your mind wandered up and down with the rows. It picked up ideas and threw them on the wagon where they piled up and all looked the same. Some of the rows were a mile long, others were a country mile. There was plenty of room. The biggest thing you could do wrong, the only felony, was to miss rocks. To skip a rock on purpose meant you were lazy and good for nothing and didn't deserve your job. There were only a few times I did that, in four summers of rock picking. No one ever caught me but Karp one time. Karp would catch you, so would Weasel Andrees.

Weasel was Worden's hired man, our foreman. He worked year round. He was the brains of the outfit and every time someone had an idea, Weasel turned it into his idea. No one liked him because he was a snitch. When he caught you skipping a rock he would tell Worden and Worden would dock you. Also, he was a sniff. He would work us through our lunch, and Worden would tell him he was a slave driver and pat him on the back. Both of them would have brown Copenhagen spit on their lips. We called that elephant snot and together they were Elephant Snot Twins. Elephant snot rolled off your lips. Weasel was a good worker because he could work all day long and not stop even to complain. Still, he was a sniff and a shitting elephant snot snitch and everyone knew it.

Karp could flanker fifteen rows past center. When Karp first started, the year after I did, Weasel kept his eyes on him, because no one could flanker that far out. But Karp never missed a rock. Weasel told Worden and Worden said it's because they were cousins, meaning Karp and the rocks.

But Karp was a big man. What he'd do out there is watch his rows and yours too, like the old hawks on Bingo Sundays at the First Farmer's Inn. If you missed one he'd just point, or else he'd even walk over to your rows to get the rock for you. If you were center on his side he was always in the corner of your eye. You'd see him point, believe me. But what made him big is when he caught someone missing a rock he wouldn't snitch. It was hard not to miss rocks because sometimes you could trip right over them, honestly, and not see them, or you'd look right at a rock and think it was a clump of dirt. If Weasel caught you skipping a clump of dirt that was really a rock he snitched, but if Karp caught you, he'd be real cool and just pick the rock up for you. He was big that way. You got to respect him after he did that enough times.

When there were too many rocks Karp said you didn't know whether to shit or go blind. In dog shit lane, the popper stopped. Dog shit lane was what we called it every time there were too many rocks. In dog shit lane Karp always said, Great. Fucking-A. Dog shit lane. Then we just bent over and picked rocks, one after another. Out beyond dog shit lane the rows were a country mile and there weren't any clouds. The dirt caked dry on our hands and we had to keep spitting on them to get a grip. Spit we called duck butter. Duck butter rolled off your tongue.

Out in those fields just after the crops began to hatch out was a lot of one color. Gray is the color of everything in the world if you've ever picked rocks. After a few hours you'd have a wagon load because the axle on the flat wagon would bow. By that time your shoes and socks and legs were gray and if you could have seen your face it would have been that color too.

The way to see another color was to follow the furrows with your eyes until they met the sky, which was sometimes blue. There were no other colors you could see really unless you closed your eyes.

After we had a load we took them to the river bed or a fence row and dropped them off. The popper didn't have a bucket so we did it by hand. It took most of an hour with a full crew. We picked up the rocks and threw them on the ground in a pile out of the way of discs. After a while you memorized where all the rock piles were by all those fields and you knew when you were getting close to one and you started to judge, by the bend in the axle, where you would stop. That kept you busy. And even though it was hard to unload the wagons, it was still a break from the walking. But after the wagon was empty you started all over again on a new row and you felt sick in your stomach because you knew how long it would take to fill that wagon up again. I guess there's nothing worse than thinking that all the work in the world is out there in front of you, and the whole time thinking, you're also smelling and seeing because it's clogging up your nose and eyes with the color gray.

When you came home at night you had to rinse off with the hose outside, or jump in Shady River before you were even allowed in the house. After dinner there was time for a little fishing or basketball, something done on your feet so you didn't get drowsy. When it was almost time for bed you went into your room, closed the door and read the feature pages of the *Bergamot Weekly Almanac*. You knew the editor there, and next summer you hoped to get hired on as a stringer. Lying in bed, you thought about the words in the rows, small and solid, and they danced in your head till you slept.

We had a convict on our crew once. After he worked all day he went to the Odette County Jail because he was on work release. Before work he had short hair the color of corn stalks in October. After a day he became all gray like the rest of us. At lunch break he would challenge us to arm wrestling on the back of the wagon. The first time, we were all ready to take him because his arms didn't look that big. They were smaller than mine, I thought, but only about half the size of Karp's and Girlie Ellefson's. Weasel took his lunch up in the metal tractor seat those days.

The convict not only said he could take us, he even bet lunch stuff he could do it in three seconds or less. That was a laugh, really, because you should have seen how puny he looked next to Karp.

Karp went down first, in two. Ellefson lasted one. I lasted maybe two. He put us down hard so the boards on the wagon shook and dust rose up. We all gave him something out of our lunch that we bet, sure we could last three. After that he laughed and told us he was an arm wrestling champion and had even won some medals in the state of Mississippi, where he grew up. He had arm wrestling and rocks in his blood, he told us, because his old man once crushed rocks on a chain gang and he had quite a strong arm, naturally. We did pretty good on account of we were going against a pro, he said.

I gave him my roast beef on wheat and pickled egg. The jail packed his lunch and he always had white bread and bologna. I always had wheat bread because my dad said white bread was like eating clouds. He put his white bread sandwich on the ground and greased it into the gray dirt with his gray boot. No one was sorry because white bread sandwich stuck to the roof of your mouth.

After that his name was Mississippi and I watched him a lot. He was happy to work because he was free then and he whistled pure music and his feet didn't sink so far in the dirt as mine. Once in dog shit lane he talked to me. Boy, you got a grip, he said. I didn't know what he was talking about at first. Then he said, You got a grip stronger than anyone out here. You'd make a good arm wrestler.

I think I was struck dumb because I didn't say anything. I just looked down for rocks in dog shit lane while he told me about arm wrestling. I made a fist in my mind.

It doesn't matter how strong your arms are. It's in your grip and in your head, Mississippi said. You gotta be sure you can take that arm and slap it down as soon as you hear go. I like to think I've got hold of an eight-pound sledge. When I hear go, all the energy in my whole body goes into my arm and into my hand. I take all that power and squeeze the sledge and swing it down. I swing it down so hard I crush whatever's in the way. I do it once with everything I got. Sometimes, I can actually see the mallet swinging through the air and my whole body becomes the handle and when the head smashes down I open my eyes and see I've won. But if I don't get it in the first seconds, it's usually over for me.

I could tell that Mississippi really had his arm wrestling figured out, and he was proud to be so good at it. A normal guy would have been proud too because most normal guys wish they had one thing they could do that well. Mississippi was quiet after he told me about arm wrestling and was speeding up his work. We were finally getting dog shit lane thinned out. Mississippi kept working faster and I could tell he was mad about something. The sweat was dripping off his nose and he looked like he might laugh. I thought that maybe he was mad because he was so good at arm wrestling, but the only place he could do it was on the back of a dusty old hay wagon or in jail and none of us could really appreciate how good he really was.

Mississippi was laughing now and as he heaved rocks at the wagon he sounded crazy. That's how you should think about arm wrestling, he said, like choking a sledge hammer handle, or choking your goddamn chicken. He couldn't stop laughing. So that's where you got your grip, he said.

There were lots of people that worked on our crew that I forgot. But I remember the convict because he gave me that compliment about my grip. I gave him my pickled eggs for a week for that. I guess you never really forget someone that's paid you a compliment like that. Even though choking your chicken sticks sideways in your throat.

There are about 2,000 steps in a mile. If you count your steps, it takes about 25 minutes to take that many, accounting for the time it takes you to stop and pick rocks. So, in a usual 10-hour day, you can walk as many as 20 miles. In 2,000 steps, you also have to pick about 50 rocks, on average. That's more than 1,000 rocks in a day, from just bigger than your fist to skull size, usually. I don't know how many rocks that is in a life or even in a year because when you're picking rocks you don't think that far ahead. One day is enough to think about. Most times that's even too much and you can break it into half days if you have a good lunch to look forward to. Half days you can break into wagon loads, wagon loads you can break into rows, rows you can break into little hills and valleys in the field and those you can break into steps. If it's one of those days, you can count the steps you need to make it over the next rise in the field. Once you get there, there's always another rise to look forward to, and if you can't make it that far there's always a big rock somewhere on the horizon that you can make it to. When it comes right down to it, there's always something you can make it to, and once you get there, something else. It's not that bad. Except you spend so much time thinking about it. You wish you could think about something better but you can't. You get the funny feeling that's why you're picking rocks.

Out there in the fields there are straight lines by the dozens. The furrows, each horizon, the train tracks by some fields, telephone poles, wires. All around you they intersect each other at odd angles. You realize that life is a straight line and you are moving along it like a slow-rolling train. Nothing can knock you off the line because you fit it perfectly. You realize that even when you're stopped you're moving along the line because it's actually pointing downhill. All you need to do is make it to the end row, turn around and come back. Make it to the end of the row, turn around and come back. That's what you do, that's what the others do, that's what the sun does. Give it up, you're going nowhere. Old Man Worden don't pay you to ponder. You see a black beard out of the corner of your eye. You look up. Karp is pointing behind you. You missed a rock. It was an accident. You were just gathering wool. Karp knows it. You pick up the rock and feel its roundness, bigger than a fist. You pitch it towards the wagon. It makes an arc in the air. You don't know where arc fits with line. You get the funny feeling that's why you're picking rocks.

We took turns driving the tractor, Weasel getting the most turns. You couldn't get me to drive the tractor. The reason is because when you were driving it, no matter who you were, you couldn't keep it going in a straight line. Before the crops began to show, that wasn't too bad. But afterwards, you always crushed some. When I crushed them I felt a little sick, even though I knew they would pop back up again with the first sprinkle.

There was one time I'll never forget that we came to the biggest rock any of us ever had to pick. It was a boulder and none us could pick it up. Worse, it was buried. I found it like you find any normal rock. There was a smooth surface in the gray, and when I kicked the rock, it wouldn't give. I bent to pick it up like you always did, but it wouldn't budge, and then I knew it was big. Someone told me once about icebergs and how they're mostly all underwater and all you can see is the tip. Well, that's what this rock was like. I couldn't get a grip on it, even when I thought about what a strong grip I had, according to what Mississippi had said. It was morning and the earth was still a little damp and some clung to my fingers. I waved to Weasel to stop the popper.

Weasel stopped and looked and I made a big circle with my arms. Weasel shook his head like he did when he wanted to show you that you were a pussy. He jumped down off the seat of the popper and grabbed the spud bar that was propped behind the tractor seat. He walked over to me and so did Karp and Girlie and Mississippi.

It's stuck, I said. It's a big one, mostly underground.

Weasel made a triangle sign over his crotch with his two thumbs and pointers. Lift it with your purse, he said. Brushing by me, he stabbed the spud bar where the rock met the dirt and it clanged on solid rock. Weasel got a shock in his funny bones and he dropped the spud bar, it vibrated so much. In a couple seconds he picked it up and went at the rock in a flurry. It was a short flurry though, and pretty soon he realized it was a really big rock. The others tried and even Mississippi couldn't budge it with his strong arm.

Karp suggested taking the popper back to the farm to get tools while everyone else worked on the rock. Weasel, the brains of the outfit, decided it would be a good idea if he took the popper back to the farm and got some more spud bars and a heavy chain. We three should stay and work on the rock. There was still mist in the air when Weasel turned the popper against the furrows and headed east, crushing the finger-high corn at every rise.

Girlie started first on the rock and didn't last too long before he said fuck the rock. He was Girlie because of his long blond hair he always wore in a ponytail. Besides picking rocks his job was to hold up the broken-down hotel in Shady Valley, the one they called the Hilton. He held it up by leaning against it all day. He was better at that job than he was at picking rocks and he probably wouldn't have lasted except that he was Karp's best friend and Karp was the best rock-picker there ever was and his only ride to work was in his best friend's beat up Chevy Nova. For the rides, Karp helped Girlie with his job nights and you could hardly drive down Main Street after dark without seeing those two with their backs against the Hilton, or else with their backs bent over that old gray Nova, trying to rise a shine on some part of it. Everyone knew it was them, even before they came completely visible as you drove down Main Street, so I guess their work paid off. Polishing a turd was what Mississippi called it when I told him what they did nights. Polishing a turd at the Hilton Hotel. It tripped the tongue.

After Girlie had his whacks, we all stood around the rock, kicking it and taking a stab with the spud bar now and then. I think it was the first time we ever stood around each other with nothing to do, so there was an awkward silence until Karp said he didn't know whether to shit or wind his wrist watch. Then we laughed until we heard the Johnny Popper coming back across the field.

Weasel brought two more spud bars, two more shovels and a chain in case we could drag it out. We set to work. First we dug around the outside of the rock. The earth was black under the upper level of gray and it was tender and crumbled. We took turns with the shovels and spud bars. Half an hour later we had exposed the sides of the boulder, which must have been six feet around. We fastened the chain around it and Weasel gave it a tug with the popper. It wiggled. After an hour we had the thing sitting free in its hole. It was as deep as it was wide and almost round. There were heaps of dirt all around us and we had dug a hole two men could stand in.

No one said anything. We were proud and sweating and the gray dirt was running down our back hollows into our pants and no one even stopped to complain. I don't think Weasel really knew what was going on. He had to look after the tractor and the crew and when work was over for us, he had to slop the hogs and do other chores. We just picked rocks. There was a big rock in the field, and because of the damage it could do to the boss's implements, it didn't belong there. Weasel sat up in the tractor where he belonged, and we were down in the dirt where we belonged.

Finally, with Weasel pulling with the tractor and Karp and Girlie down in the hole prying, the giant rock popped out of its nest. We were all covered in gray and sweat and just stood around the thing, sitting there on top of the ground. You wondered what was inside of it. It looked like some giant bird had come and dropped its black egg in the middle of the field. Karp made the joke about the turd in the punchbowl.

With more prying and tugging we managed to roll the big egg on top of a dirt pile so it was even with the back of the wagon. With all four of us taking hold, we heaved it on. The wagon boards complained and the axle bowed. It was a full load.

When you saw it sitting there on the wagon, it looked better than a whole wagon load of those smaller rocks. I think everyone else felt the same because we just stood around it and admired. Mississippi broke the silence. Just look at that mother would you.

You felt like you had done a job, a real job, and when Weasel said it was still an hour until lunch and we should get back to work you wouldn't have known it was so late because it seemed like the day had just started. Karp and Girlie plunked down where they were and didn't look like they were ready to do anything. When Weasel said, sternly, Let's move it, Mississippi squatted next to them.

Mississippi. Now there was a name. More hills and hollows than six normal names. And it belonged to a convict with a sledge hammer arm. Who knew what he would do.

In those situations you have to do something to keep everything going on like it should. Weasel sat up on the tractor and you could tell he was thinking of how much to dock us. The popper smelled like burning oil after its workout and the rest of the crew stayed put. The big rock was sitting up on the wagon and just then I decided that the whole world was made out of rocks and that if you picked up all the rocks in a field there would be more there the next year because the ground just kept pushing them up and steel disc harrows just kept digging for them and if you were a rock picker you might as well buck up and live with it.

You do what you can. I just mentioned that we should take a dip, get some of the grime off. Maybe we could roll the big rock into Shady River and dive off it. The river's not far.

Weasel might have just saved his work crew for the season when he called from the tractor for us to knock off for lunch. It was the heat of the day and, hell, we should take a dip, get some of the grime off. The river's not far. We might even roll the big sombitch in for a diving rock.

After driving across the field, he backed the wagon up to the river and we shoved the load off. The boulder fell easily, mowed down the weeds on the way to the river and sank quiet as a bottom fish into a deep hole. After that we got ready to swim.

You'd be surprised that it really isn't that easy for men to get undressed in front of each other. Karp was on one side of the tractor, Girlie the other. Weasel was up in his seat. Mississippi went behind the wagon and I tumbled into the weeds. When we all walked out, naked except for our underwear, carrying our clothes in front of ourselves, it was our feet that you noticed first. Compared to our gray calves, our ankles looked like brand new pairs of white socks. But that was nothing compared to the shock you got when the work boots and dirty clothes hit the dirt. Our underwear was a rainbow. Karp's were blue. They stood out against his white and hairy beer belly. Mississippi's were green, Girlie's orange, Weasel's yellow and mine red. They weren't the kind of bright colors you would hope for if you were hoping for color. These underwear were a good two years off the X-Mart discount rack, and they were stretched and faded from two years of grunt work. Of course there were some rips in the wrong places, but besides that, they'd held up well.

If you happened to be driving down Hemlock Hollow Road that day around noontime, and if you looked to the west over the gray mass that was Harlan Worden's largest field, you might have seen what looked like, to the naked eye, a flock of slow moving, somewhat faded Toucan Sams, dousing themselves in the muddy waters of Shady River. If someone told you that was Worden's rock crew you wouldn't have believed them. I couldn't believe it, either, how the color was always right there in those men.

Long Range Forecast

Everybody knows that the ratio of black bristles to rust on the woolly bear caterpillar foretells the coming winter. More black bristles mean a hard winter; more rust, a mild one. Or maybe it's the other way around. It scarcely matters...if you distrust the augury of a given woolly bear, then you simply ignore that caterpillar, take a step, and believe another.

—*The Old Farmer's Almanac*, 2011

Barnyard Billy
Licks the Grass

Billy can throw a baseball. He can milk cows. He can bring his old man a beer. Billy's cow barn faces Hemlock Hollow. The barn's road side is white in new tin siding. Its corrugated teeth glisten white. The barn's business side is worn wood siding. Red like any old barn. Billy picks a plank and beans it. Pretty soon, Billy blisters the wood, and he picks another plank and beans that one. The baseballs make axe strokes on the wood, and these sounds reverberate over Hemlock Hollow, grazing the alfalfa tops and nestling among the purple clover.

Billy has a baseball arm, you can be sure of it. He can nail the silver silo top with a rock sure as rain, and the silver silo top has tiny dimples that smile in the sun. Billy's small white farmhouse rests along the dirty red road that leads to the barn. Necklace to the house is the clothesline where his mother hangs the family's little clothes, the tiny white pearls.

Billy's fifteen, and he's a man already. Proof: he has a man's beard, chews a man's tobacco, works a man's day. When you take a drive across Odette County you see boys like Billy in the fields driving tractors too soon. You don't live out there, out on the land, but you've never been too far away. And you don't need to be in search of a story to take notice to things out there, boys like Billy. You might just wonder what they feel or dream. You might wonder if they're little boys on Tonka toys only playing grown. Billy drives his tractor across Hemlock Hollow past the lone remaining hemlock to the high alfalfa field.

You might see Billy in the summer cutting hay. Come fall you might see Billy out there spreading manure. If you pass him enough times you may cease to wonder, the way you get used to things. When you pass him enough times you may forget to see, and Billy may become scenery, some old implement already rusting on the horizon.

Billy in the barnyard. Billy in the field. Drive into Bergamot and stop down to Hoosie's Best Shot, you might see Billy in the tavern. He'll be with his old man, Bill Sr. They'll be shooting pool or leaning over an Old Style chewing fat with gray-haired Hoosie. You might want to ask Billy about his rifle arm. Interview him about his sport and he'll say fuck baseball, just loud enough so his old man can hear. At fifteen, Billy knows baseball is a boy's game. He finds out from his father every time he puts on his sissy tights and shitless, ass-white ball cap. You like playing faggot, Billy? Bill Sr. says. You like playing sissy stick while your old man busts ass?

Get on the subject of baseball, and Bill Sr. starts in on other things. He and Hoosie might lay into Billy about Kitty Wetnight, the shy harelip girl who lives down to the old Valley Cheese Co-op. The shabby, cinder block cheese factory's just a house now, like most of the farms around here, but it's home to Billy's girl. Bill Sr. tells Hoosie all about it. I think Billy here's giving it to that harelip, he says. My boy here's finally looked out past the calf huts and look what catches his eye. Hoosie pours another frothy Old Style and tells the old man that's just how it is. A man's gotta dip his wick someplace, Hoosie says, giving Billy a wink and sliding him a beer. A bucket's a bucket.

Billy sits and waits for the talk to turn back to farming. He grips the frosty beer mug so tight it begins to sweat around his fingers. It's all in good fun, he knows. If you're tough like a real farmer, you can take it. Billy will be a farmer; ask him and he'll tell you, just loud enough. It makes you sick to hear about it, and if you know Billy you'd like to set him straight before he's too far gone. You'd like to take him by the shoulders, shake him and say, Goddamn Billy, take a look around. You farm and you'll be an old broke-down shit spreader piled on a bar stool or crapped out on one of them hills. Look at these farms falling down around here. Pick up that baseball. Pick up that baseball, Barnyard, and don't put it down!

But Barnyard Billy doesn't have the kind of shoulders you can shake. You see the bull in that kid and know a good brass nose ring is the only way to lead him. You'd like to take hold of that brass ring, twist it good, and lead Billy out beyond the cow yard for a change.

Oh, Billy plays baseball, but not like you'd like. Billy on the ball field knows he is better than the other boys—teammates or opponents—who can't tell a Holstein from a Hereford. Billy is pitcher. He hurls the pearl. And when he's on the mound he can see the other boys' fear. They stand back off home plate and twitch nervously, like heifers first locked in the stanchion. Billy can see them quiver. He doesn't soothe them like he soothes a nervous heifer. Sometimes he pitches them high inside just so he can watch them jump away from the plate. Billy is wild. He either strikes the other boys out or beans them. He works up a sweat out there, and the cowhide becomes smooth as skin under his slippery fingers. Sometimes he loses one completely, and it goes careening over the backstop. The boys live in fear of being beaned by Billy. Their mothers sit in the stands and hate Billy, that bully. Their fathers wish their sons were Billy, both for his rifle arm and for his loyalty to dear old Dad.

Billy's pearl is a blistering pain for the other boys. The number ninety-four is attached to his fastball half across county. Ninety-four miles per hour. Everyone knows Billy can throw a ball ninety-four miles per hour. Grownups throw the number ninety-four back and forth across bulk tanks or over bar tops. Boys whisper ninety-four into their lockers and across lunch tables. They want nothing to do with that kind of speed. Boys' mothers want Billy put in a separate league. Scouts from University, reporters from your bigger papers— they all get lost driving past Hemlock Hollow again and again, looking frantically for Billy's house and school. Billy, you could guess, has no other pitch. Finesse is for faggots, he would have learned to say by now.

You love to see Billy pitch, the way he works. He has fast and that's it. He doesn't cheat. He saves nothing, throws each pitch like it's his last. Spends it, shoots it, loses it. And at the next pitch finds more. After Billy strikes the boys out, or beans them, or loses the ball over the backstop, he goes on home to chores. He doesn't stay on the diamond to practice drills with his teammates. He has cows to milk. Mornings it's Billy driving the old man's pickup to school after chores, late most days. After school, Kitty Wetnight rides the bus home while Billy stays and throws for awhile. He has this arrangement with Coach: he can chew tobacco; he need not stay for all of practice; on game days, he need only throw. Billy chews, spits, throws, trucks home to chores.

Billy alone after chores pitches against the dusky barn back. In his mind he is vaguely rehearsing for some big game. He steps off the 20 paces and goes to work. He has one ball, throws it, hears the axe whack wood, the sound cleave the mow, echo out beyond the barn. He walks and picks up. Billy winds up. He doesn't see Feller or Koufax or Gibson when he winds up. Farmers don't have heroes. Billy sees only the barn plank and he throws the ball. He aims at the smudge his first pitch has made, and soon that slight smudge is surrounded by a herd of others: cows out around the silage bin, an occasional stray. Billy has been at this a long while, and the back of the barn is dotted with these groupings, each its own solar system. Billy aims at the center of the new one he's making. He aims beyond it. As he throws he's splitting firewood and aiming behind the wood at the chopping block. Beyond the barn plank is the mow. Billy aims beyond the barn plank at the hay bales he can see in his mind. Each pitch piles into the barn and splinters the wood. He imagines his fastball blasting through the wood and burrowing into the eighty-pound bales he had stacked squarely and securely in the mow.

It is darkening and Billy throws by the cow-yard light. He unloads again and again. He works up a light lather and gives off a sheen under the light as each magnificent fastball falls sweaty and smooth below the weather-beaten back of the barn.

Billy is Bill Jr. First son. Bill Sr. is Billy's only hero. Billy has young twin brothers, Curtis and Cletus; they're eleven. Billy is God to his smaller brothers. To them he can throw a rock into orbit, and you better not arm wrestle him or he'll break your wrist. Billy is a beacon to these boys, a silo top, something to aim for. Billy does morning chores alone and lets his brothers sleep in.

Mornings in the barn find Billy alone with the herd and the noises of the barn: the radio, the vacuum pump, the complacent mooing. He is enamored of his skill and floats among the cows almost without effort. Billy has been doing this for a long while. He has a knack for repetition. Already he can shut his mind down and concentrate only on repeating the same movements. For Billy, milking cows is like baseball, and neither is a team sport. He is at his best like this, working alone, and he has the same dreams as anyone: of someday having twice the cows in twice the barn. He checks the dipstick in the bulk tank to see how much milk he has coaxed. Someday he will make twice the milk.

Billy trucks off to school. He's not embarrassed for the smell of cow barn and wears it to Bergamot High like some banner. Some days when Billy's on time he swings by the old cheese factory to pick up Kitty Wetnight. He finds her outside draping the clothesline with a load of clean whites. Then she disappears briefly into the cheese factory. Waiting in the driveway, he can see her flitting back and forth behind the thick glass bricks that are the cheese factory windows. Billy clears the baling twine, beer cans and stray wrenches from the bench seat to make a clean place for Kitty. She wears a flowered dress and smells like sweet cream when she gets in. She closes the door carefully on the old pickup, treating it like a delicate thing. They sit up straight in the cab. Billy drapes a sweaty hand at twelve o'clock on the wheel. He trucks Kitty to school and carries her books to class.

The bravest of the boys at school call him Barnyard Billy, though not to his face, and they say Old Barnyard puts it to Kitty in the bed of the pickup before school. The bravest of the girls talk about the feel of his strong hands and strong arm. They watch Billy truck into school with Kitty and whisper that she's only keeping the seat warm for them. They agree they'd take it—for a night.

Sometimes Billy shares a lunch table with Kitty, and when you walk by, the smell of cow barn mingles pleasantly there with baby Swiss. In class, Billy sits quiet. He grips the sweaty desktop to withstand the battery of words like geometry and evolution and velocity. He holds tight through the day, and after school at practice he unleashes a barrage of fastballs that pound back at the school everything that was pounded at him. After he pitches he drives home with a limp hand resting on Kitty's empty place.

Then it's Billy in the barn again. Evening chores are for the whole family, except Ma. They milk late, after dinner. When you drive past Billy's farm on Hemlock Hollow you see the barn lights on late most nights. There are other farms out here on these gaunt, curving roads with their barn lights on late too, compressors still pumping indecently: light and noise eerie in the darkness. You know what this means. You know what happens when a farmer works in his barn half the night. If you've been in Billy's barn, or one like it, you know how it goes. Things begin on cue. Bill Sr. calls the cows in, and the twins lock them in their stanchions. Then he and his oldest boy read the breeding wheel: who's fresh, who's dry, and who's yet to be bred back in. Bill Sr. re-marks the treated cows, sets up the milk house, and then his work is done. He's got the boys trained what to do next, just like his dad trained him. The neighbor, Harlan Worden, comes over after his chores to drink a beer with Bill Sr. The two have faded bibs and matching beer guts. They drain a few, and then the fun starts.

The twins become like two roosters in the hen house. Bill Sr. eggs them on. Together he and Harlan egg the boys on while Billy changes most of the milk machines himself. Who's got the bigger rooster of you boys? Harlan says.

Curt's bigger, but Clete has more hair, Bill Sr. responds. Ain't that right Clete? Ain't your brother got his old man's pecker? Ain't you got a little furry one like fairy-pants Billy?

Down the aisle, beneath a cow, Billy doesn't even flush. He knows the twins are ashamed, but they're used to it. They know what to expect. Eventually they're coaxed into a fight by the old man. Hey Clete, Curt here says you're up all night chokin' on your chicken. Curt here says you try to climb into his bed and touch his. You gonna let your brother cluck like that?

The twins don't look at each other when they fight. They look at the ground mostly. Pretty soon they're rolling in the aisle, getting dusted in barn lime, arms and legs flying. They swing wildly, but there are no hits to the face. One of the dogs, the black and white heeler mutt, starts to bark and nip. Some country song comes in loud and clear on the radio. The cows get restless in their stanchions, and Billy rests his head and a hand against their flanks as he works beneath them. They comfort each other like this.

Put him in the shit! Harlan eggs. He's getting excited and his beer starts to foam over. Stick his face in it! Harlan kicks the dog and the heeler scampers out. At his old man's direction, Billy gets out from under a cow, brings him and Harlan a fresh Old Style from the milk house. The three stand around and watch the twins roll close to the gutter, just grazing the green shit. One rolls onto Bill Sr.'s massive hobnailed work boots. Ow! Ow! My foots! he cries.

Billy has his own big feet. He is on the man's side, but really he wants to get down and roll near the shit with his brothers. To show them you can grow up from there. Their faces turn bright red, and they struggle and begin to cry, coming dangerously near the shit-full gutters and their massive chain cleaners. The adults whoop it up. Look at the shit twins! Harlan shouts. I can't tell 'em apart.

Finally, Bill Sr.'s had enough and gives Billy the nod. Billy reaches down with his strong baseball arm and snatches one brother off the other. They get up, but stare at the ground. Looks like Clete here kicked your ass, Curt, Bill Sr. says. Maybe you ought to whack off like him or you'll always suck the hind tit. That's how they'll tell it down to Hoosie's: 'Curtsey Curt sucks the hind tit.' Harlan is doubled over laughing, and Billy looks off down the row of cows to the barn door. The door is rectangular, longer than it is tall. He looks off to the darkening west pasture. How do you think big brother got his strong arm? Bill Sr. says. The boys don't move. Suddenly the barn radio loses its noise. Oh, all right, go on off and cry to Mommy, the father says, and the boys file out.

With the twins gone, it's Billy's turn until chores are done. Billy works while the two men drink and blabber. Billy sees some of the cows' teats are calloused from the abuse of the milk machines, and he applies udder balm to soften them. He then dips them gently in the red antiseptic. When the men finish a beer one will shout, Hey, boy! and Billy will go to the milk house and fetch a beer. See how he's trained? Bill Sr. says to Harlan.

So Harlan tries one: Boy! Lick my boots!

Billy tells Harlan to go fuck a dead pony. Then it's Bill Sr. who's doubled over laughing. Harlan says, What? He gulps his beer and crushes the can in his fist.

After chores, Billy flushes the pipeline, cleans the milk machines and unclips the cows. They shoulder out into the darkness of the west pasture. He shuts the compressor down and walks uphill toward the house. Billy decides to skip ball practice tonight. It has gotten late. He notices the sky is chalked with stars: a million tiny baseballs just out of reach.

He picks a rock and flings it split-fingered toward the night, hears it fall short.

Inside, Billy shucks his boots and bibs on the porch, careful not to muddy the clean kitchen linoleum. He kisses his mother, reading a romance there in the kitchen. I'll be up soon, she says. He climbs the creaking stairs to the attic room he shares with the twins. He finds them asleep in the same bed again. They're curled together like blind baby field mice. Billy has to pry their warm bodies apart, and he carries Cletus over to his own single bed. The boy doesn't wake up, but curls up tighter when touched. Billy tucks his brother in. He undresses and climbs into his own bed, curling there against the cold sheets.

The dark room is shot with feeble moonlight from the window facing the barn. Billy looks out. He can see the milk house light still on. Through the small perfect square of the milk house window he can see his father's and Harlan's arms pass over the bulk tank. They seem to be arm wrestling. Billy feels his own strong arm under the covers and wonders where it came from. You didn't lick it off the grass, be sure of that, his old man tells him. You have me to thank, and this farm. You think you'd have a strong arm if I didn't put you to squeezing cow tits? You be thankful of what I give you. Billy says his thanks and begins to drift away. He imagines his father coming in the house, walking sock-footed and bib-less over his mother's spotless linoleum. His father's feet look small.

Then Billy hears someone begin to creak up the attic stairs. It is Kitty snuck out of the cheese factory, Billy thinks. His hands sweat. Then he comes to, fathoms his mistake. It is his mother come to say goodnight. She is heavy, and he can see clearly now an image of her struggling up the smooth wooden stairs, grasping the smooth, damp handrail, creaking. This nightly trip is a burden for her, he knows, and he counts each creak become louder. She seems to be coming from someplace far away. He listens as the sounds carry her closer.

*   *   *   *   *

If you drive on out to Billy's house on an early Saturday afternoon, you ought to know enough to drive right past the house and grinning clothesline to park in front of the barn. No one but Billy's ma will be in the house. Her kitchen window looks out to the barn, and you can turn and wave at her as you get out of the truck and head into the barn. She'll be there. In the barn you're liable to find the twins laying down feed or scraping the aisle. You'll note they're respectful, fine-looking boys. Ask and they'll say directly that Dad and Billy are out working on the old Oliver, or fixing the drive chain on the shit spreader what's gummed up with twine. Walk up the red gravel lane, and you get a view of the place unseen from the road. You notice the outbuildings: decrepit and decaying, barely tethered, their pocked tin roofs rusting through and sagging where the trusses have given, their windows opaque, cobwebbed and splintered. You notice how everything is cobbled together with baling twine: the door of the hog shed, the feed crib, the shit-slathered calf huts. Out in the yard retired tires, a broken hay rake, a leaking planter all sit like sculpture where they first collapsed, now homes for nesting birds and mice who make hay with all the twine strands and occasional red thread from another battered baseball. The very withers of the whole place seem to sag sad-ass down to its haunches, everything draped in a funeral wreathe of unraveling twine, waiting for a swift wind to carry it, some old banner, out over Hemlock Hollow below.

Find the tractor out behind the machine shed and you'll find Senior and Junior hunkered into the guts of her. Watch them and you'll begin to understand the delicate circuitry of this life. The distributor's wet, Bill Sr. says. If the distributor's wet, the old sow won't turn over. Billy looks on as his dad continues. Check to see if the plugs are fouled and won't fire.

As Billy checks the plugs, his father's greasy fingers move deftly in the heart of the old pig, following the wires from one dilapidated organ to the next, searching for this week's ailment. We'll see if the starter's shot, he says. Lay your screwdriver across it like this. If we get spark, we can start her up that way, but we'll need a new crank for the old sow eventually.

When they finally get the old Oliver running, Billy hooks up to the spreader and they haul out to Hemlock Hollow to spread the shit. Billy drives and Bill Sr. rides along on the fender. They seem to delight that the old tractor's running so well on all her pistons. The rebuilt two-barrel makes a thutthutthut that almost passes for music. Bill Sr. lights a smoke and looks out over the field. He passes it over to Billy who takes a drag. You can watch the two bouncing along on the old tractor, getting smaller with distance, some of the farm dogs trailing behind, the old man reaching over his boy to nudge the throttle and engage the power take off. The PTO adds a whirr to the thutthutthut and these sounds curve through the long valley and hasten back again. You can watch the ragged teeth of the old spreader grind into a spin, bite into the cow manure at its mouth and spray the wet manure gradually in a thin, glistening green fan out over the midday pasture.

You can see that after they finish spreading manure, they shut her down and sit awhile, out by the shade tree. You don't know what they're talking about. If you watch from the cow yard, by where the milk truck backs in, or if you drive by the fresh-paved road and take a gander out over Hemlock Hollow, you see them there. You don't live out here, out on the land, but sometimes you'd like to. For a moment, you wish that was you out on the field. If only you could be close enough to hear what they say. Likely they just sit like you do after a chore is done and there's time to kill—when the pleasure of finishing a job isn't spoiled yet with the thought of starting another one. Watching, you see the old man's arm rise up as he points to something happening somewhere on his acreage. You wish you were close to him then. Close to his motley whiskers, dirty seed cap and tobacco-filled lip. So close that you could smell the fermented silage as you looked along the flannel barrel of his arm, out beyond his hard and crooked finger, to see where he was pointing.

This is life on Hemlock Hollow. You put cows out to pasture, finish up chores, and then wait awhile as the small clod of earth unfurls. The cows low in the pasture and drink in the small creek that flows through. Turkey vultures rise over the pasture and see themselves briefly in the creek. There are trout in the creek that fear the shadows of the vultures and peg-legged egrets. The trout covet a new hatch of mayflies aflutter in a haze over the stream, but the scared fish cower in their watery riffles. Bronze water boatmen skate bravely on the water's veneer. Muskrats steer downstream mouthing succulent willow shoots. The twins have snuck like weasels from the barn and followed the cows out to pasture. They soak a worm in the creek's deep hole and wait for a nibble. Likely as not they'll fetch out a chub, squeeze its eyes gently out and hunker back among the nettles.

The boys chew on crab grass, smoke a stolen cigarette and spy on their bobbers. There is time to kill. The cows won't come back in to milking until Farmer Bill opens the cow yard gate and calls to them with his deep bullfrog bassoon. HereBossBossBoss. EeereBooooss. HeyooBooss. Then cows will come nose to fetlock in a single file that curves safely around the clusters of brambles. They will step daintily into the creek, their full udders carrying their chapped teats downward to tingle in the coolness of the creek and linger teasingly there those few precious steps.

You look out and see Billy looking where his old man points. His eyes are trained on something all right. But a sudden covey of white butterflies arises somewhere between here and there, obscuring your vision of him. Then the rare pause is diminished, and as sure it's time to move on. As days do, this one begins to tilt toward sunset already.

It's a Saturday afternoon in June and Barnyard Billy's season is running out on him. He has an inkling of some big game looming in the moist air over Hemlock Hollow, and he waits for it to settle among the clover where he can get his best hand on it, wrap two fingers around the seam that binds it. Meantime his ma waits for the wash cycle to run out, and his old man waits again for chores time and Harlan Worden to come swaggering on in with another twelver to wash down a day. The twins hide out by the creek, or up in the mow, waiting all afternoon for bedtime and a chance to curl together. Down the road Kitty Wetnight waits distorted behind thick glass for another ride to happen by.

You wish you could holler to them all: Come out! Come out! And that they would each step forth from the scenery and stop their waiting. You'd like to help them take the clothes in off the line and get on with it. Tell Billy he's had his big game already. Last year you may have been in the stands to see it. Or you may have read about it here in the *Almanac*, about how he struck out twenty in a no-hitter over seven and still managed to lose 3-2 on walks. You took your best shot Billy, and you missed. You're not gonna be some smart-ass college punk. But Billy doesn't know that was his big game. He still thinks the big one's just around the bend. The big one that'll change everything: each year it gets smaller with memory.

But what if he hasn't had his big game? How will he know it when it comes to pass? What has he to do but wait on it? Stare down each day like it's another skinny batter. Shake off the dim-witted catcher who so wants Billy to mix up his pitches, if only to give his own throbbing mitt a rest. Billy's got no other pitch. He spits tobacco juice, rears back, and comes with everything. Gives all to each. He wants to throw so hard he cuts clean through the wood to the chopping block, so he'll know it finally—what's behind it all. He wants his fastball to rip the catcher's mitt clean off at the wrist, to see the connecting matter. He'd like just to wheel around and fire one out past the sky into orbit, just because he can. Throw it up there to take its place with the other starry millions.

And Billy will one day. Billy with that throw. Billy on the mound. Billy the diamond. What if that's his pitch, the big one? What if that pitch comes from nowhere, licked from the very grass? What if he feels that pitch flee his moist fingers like no other has? What if he watches down the barrel of his strong arm as the fine pearl hurtles toward the sky, toward the curve of the horizon? What if it curves into the very orbit? And what if we—the whole lot of us—were on hand to watch? What if we, and the twins, and Bill Sr. and Ma, and Kitty Wetnight could all watch together—watch the red thread loosen, the leather cover begin to flap in the wind, the thread unwinding with the spin and curve of the ball, trailing away behind it, and what if we all lost track of it together for the brightness?

We'd file out of the stands that day knowing we'd seen something, each of us returning to our own cows and to our own patch of grass with a sense of wonder. Sure chores time will come again. But Barnyard Billy gives us pause. Billy's new pitch is hope. We'll all of us promise to keep an eye out for that kid, hoping to preserve some moment of him, lest he rust away into scenery before our eyes.

Horseface Cunningham Breaks His Maiden

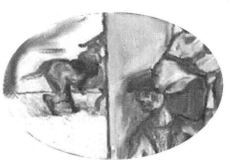

Cunningham grew up on a long and winding gravel road that has since been paved and straightened. At the ends of Blood's Point Road, and in between, lay everything that Cunningham knew anything about at all. At one end, his coop: former chicken house turned Cunningham house. His farmhouse and barnyard bulldozed, his mangy family blown about like dandelion whispers, Cunningham stayed behind to live alone in the sole remaining outbuilding—among the poop and feathers—afraid that too might be flattened in the night. Good odds, if not, that snot-freezing, ball-bluing winter would barge in early. Just sixteen, Cunningham was already a dropout, an orphan, and a bachelor. To pass time and crush want nights after work, he read fairy tales by candle light or looked at picture books about big places in the world. He sounded out and committed to his chicken-coop memory the big words in the captions under the pretty pictures. *App-a-loo-sa. Ar-e-thu-sa. An-thro-po-mor-phism.*

At the other end of that gravel road sat a badly-aged thoroughbred farm called Flax Ranch with a half-mile dirt training track that looped around the slanted buildings and weedy grounds. This was Cunningham's workplace, a kingdom with its own queen and princess. A peeling and tottering oak fence—bowed between its posts—still managed to girdle the overgrown acreage. On a blue-sky summertime day the yellow dandelions and coveted purple clover, alive with burly honey bees, bruised the greenish pasture and made a sublime collage of wildness and decay. Inside the track, the thoroughbreds and boarder horses grazed shoulder to shoulder in their separate paddocks within the oaked-in pasture. On cool summer mornings the thoroughbreds looked splendid but nervous in their colorful blankets while the boarder horses stood naked, nose to tail, calmly swatting the just-awakening black flies and no-see-ums from their partners' scalloped Arabian faces.

First thing mornings in the horse barn, Cunningham fed and watered the thoroughbreds. It wasn't quite light, and Cunningham worked by the dull yellow glow of the cobwebbed bulbs lining the aisle along the horse stalls. Assaulting his ears were the neighs, whinnies and grunts of the hungry beasts. There were twenty stalls in all, each housing an athletic thoroughbred, and Cunningham ran half a bucket of well water for each animal. Shadowing Cunningham at his work was a white, blue-eyed barn cat that had turned up overnight, like some habits do. He named the white puss El Salvador, fed it dog food. Salvador followed Cunningham as a dog would, watching him expectantly. The cat's presence seemed to have a calming effect on the horses. Nights Salvador slept on an old saddle in the gloomy tack room.

Cunningham walked the aisle, bid good morning to the horses and stroked their soft chins, which relaxed like dewlaps at his touch. He liked to fit his shoulder up under the muzzles of the horses and feel the weight of their heads on his shoulder as he rubbed their chins and cooed into their feathery ears. Yet groggy with morning, the high-strung horses still allowed themselves to be groped and coddled.

Horses watered, Cunningham fed. He peeled two thin flakes of alfalfa for each animal. He put these flakes in the hay cribs fastened to each stall wall. By the time the twentieth horse was fed, the first was done eating and Cunningham began the slow process of leading the horses one by one to their paddocks so he could muck and grain each of the stalls. If the morning was cool or wet he would blanket the horses before leading them out into the gray weather.

Cunningham knew which horses couldn't tolerate each other so that, for example, Miss Slew and Young Wife had to be in separate paddocks, while Mission Bells could sidle up to Oh's Profit, but only so long as Seminary Queen was with him. Separating the finicky purebreds made double the trouble for Cunningham, and sometimes, despite his affection for the animals, he daydreamed about putting them all out to pasture together so they could battle out their *hauteur* and *chauvinism* as *gladiators* at *Circus*.

Cunningham daydreamed also about riding the animals. He loved to ride, and here he was working at a barn where he couldn't mount any of the horses. He thought it must be something akin to a wagon-riding rummy taking a job at a liquor store. Oh the temptation. Oh, to fall face first from the wagon, from the steed, into the liquory slop of equine bliss. But there were other temptations on this farm as well, and despite his mundane job, Cunningham was no clock watcher. He managed to spend most of the day excited and tingly, sometimes finding himself erect at the oddest times, like while alone in a dirty stall, silage fork in hand, or sitting on the tractor, bucket high, dropping a load of dirty arena shavings into the dump truck. And there, when he snapped-to, would be Salvador, virgin white, watching him accusingly, purring: *derelict, pervert.*

At times like those Cunningham cursed his size. He was six-foot tall and weighed a solid two-twenty. A good portion of his weight was anchored in his hind quarters. You are a big boy, his mother had told him. Put down that crop and pick up a shovel. You will work like a horse, not ride one. He had fifty pounds too many to train the delicate thoroughbreds, and he had passed the ideal jockey weight four years and eighty-some pounds ago, when he was twelve. Curse his size. To be a runt. To never have to duck. To be birdlike and sprightly. To be willowy and bow wheat-like in the breeze. Oh.

One of Cunningham's chicken coop books was given him by Romero. It was a fairy tale about a bulky young pauper who ate some funny seeds to become so small he crept into the ear of this magical wild stallion and crept out the other ear a dashing, elf-like prince named Vasquez The Small But Mighty. Then there was this contest, and the young pauper and his steed jumped, on the third try, all the way up to the top story of this castle, and the princess, living up there beyond the trellises, gave him a rose that she had been holding tirelessly in her teeth. The crowd oohed and aahhed at the grace and nimbleness of the princely pauper, and he was given the princess's hand in Catholic matrimony. He never had to be poor, nor grubby, nor bulky, nor alone again. It was a Cinderella story for big dull farmboys Cunningham supposed, and it suited him just right. He often imagined finding funny seeds to eat so he could be horse-ear sized like Vasquez The Small But Mighty from the fairytale. Magic seeds consumed, he would climb in the horse's ear using a machete to clear away the sticky quack grass and stalky cattails of the equine inner ear. It was dark in there, and humid. Always before he found his way around the horse's small but lumpy brain he would awaken from his reverie, embarrassed and big as ever, holding a silage fork instead of a machete.

The piss-soaked straw could be quite rancid, and sometimes the horses slopped their buckets, mixing piss and water with apples in the straw. Cunningham thanked the neat horses who pissed and shit all in one corner, and cursed the slobs who strew and stomped their excrement all over the stall. Cunningham was a whiz at mucking stalls. He learned the technique from Romero, the gallant Mexican trainer who used to work here with him. Romero knew horses, boy, and he could pick a winner just by running his hand from a horse's rump to fetlock. Romero taught him how to turn the dirty straw and pick out the apples and wetness in two cat-like motions, flicking the mess into the two-wheeled cart.

It was easy to see that Romero had intimate, perhaps mystical knowledge of horses, and Cunningham paid close attention to what he said. Cunningham tried to perfect Romero's mucking instructions, and often he found himself concentrating so hard on mucking a stall quickly and efficiently that he would forget having done a dozen or more, a whole hour gone by without his wherewithal. He would find himself quite embarrassed that he had put so much thought and effort into doing something as stupid and meaningless and easy as mucking a stall. He, who once brandished masterfully the riding crop he found in Grandpa's trunk. Like Romero's ebony crop. Romero. Where for went thou Romero, with thy broken back, soiled britches and *cabesa mas fina*? Cunningham. What will thy do, Cunningham? Live in thine coop and pitch horse apples thy lonely life through? Yon bulldozers belcheth. Gray houses encroacheth. Go forth and get a real live job like thine father, Cunningham.

The stable boy had mucked most kinds of shit already in his life: horse, cow, chicken, pig, bull. And then he'd shoveled dirt, concrete (which they called mud), snow in the winter, as well as sand when Shady River by the old farmstead rose. Anything that took a strong back. But he guessed he liked shoveling horse shit just about best. It had a pleasant aroma when it was blended nicely with straw, or even by itself, away from the rancid pisswater mix. Yes, horse shit suited him just fine. Much less caustic or drippy than chicken.

And Cunningham liked how the horse shit and straw mix made a moldering pile out in the pasture due to internal combustion, so the pile never seemed to get any bigger, even though he heaped on several loads every day. Some things in the world were amazing how they worked, and it made Cunningham happy to think about them, but it made him feel stupid too, that he never understood just why or how things managed to happen.

When he was finished mucking stalls, Cunningham loaded fresh straw bales in the two-wheeled cart and trundled them across the grounds from the mow to the horse barn where he freshened each stall with new, dry straw. Next he used the cart to carry sweet feed in to the stalls, and he parceled out a scoop and a half to each horse, giving a little more to his favorites, like Purple Moment, gimpy in the leg, and Want Crusher, and a little less to such messy nags as Harlot's Hair and Nonnie Nellie. Cunningham loved the sweet feed, the sticky smell and feel of the molasses on the corn and oats. He often ate a little himself—though it never tasted as good as it smelled—and he'd let out a whinny, just to be funny. Cunningham always kept a pocketful of sweet feed, which assured he'd have friends among the horses. The sweet feed was octane boost to the horses, and they'd be wound up tightly by the time Fern came in to ride.

Cunningham checked the digital clock by the water pump and saw that he was ahead of schedule. He had half an hour to get the horses back into their stalls and let them eat so Fern could come and ride the snot and lather out of them. You couldn't bring the horses in like you brought in cows. The job had to be done one at a time, which was no easy chore because the edgy horses all gathered near the barn door, expecting their oats.

Cunningham emerged with the red and green lead. One by one he budged the horses into their stalls until only Want Crusher remained by the sliding barn door. Want Crusher, you dream. Such a patient horse, and mannerly. Dappled gray in a herd of bay. She was big and beautiful and fast too, recently showing against 7-1 at Arlington. He clipped the red and green lead on her emerald halter and let her nuzzle around wetly by his pants pockets for a taste of feed while he led her to her stall. Knowing he had the horse's attention, he swung up onto the animal's back and lay there, cheek to twitching withers, hand-feeding the sticky morsels and feeling the rippling muscles beneath his groin. You are a horse fly, Cunningham, hold tight. He imagined racing her to victory, mouth and hands full of mane floss, his body coaxing every drop of performance from her, riding hard, the crowd cheering and Want Crusher heaving. Oh. Ladies and gentlemen, a first in the history of our sport. A big jockey. Look at the size of him. What a load! Could it be a new trend? Is Want Crusher the better and stronger for her big rider? Or are her delicate bones turning to meal for hefting that tonnage around the mile track? Time will tell, ladies and gentlemen. Life is short and horse racing long; let us enjoy the spectacle.

When Want Crusher finally protested his dotings, Cunningham slid off, sweaty, embarrassed, feeling that familiar ebb and pulse of satisfaction and yearning. And there was Salvador, Salvadoro Blanco, above him on the stall wall—

his swallow-hunting perch—looking down at him. Screw you, Salvador. Scat.

Nine-thirty. Break time for Cunningham. Time for Fern's dramatic entrance. Cunningham quickly saddled and haltered the horse in Stall One. Then he planted himself on a stray bale, fixed a little dish of dog chow for Salvador, forgiven, who ate from his lap. Cunningham poured some warm coffee from his stained silver thermos, lit a cig from his rumpled pack, waited, smoked and drank. The polite sounds of Salvador's eating mingled with the grain grinding noises emanating from the clean, happy stalls.

Fern was heiress to the broken-down ranch. Dirty blonde, daughter to Roxanne (there was a woman, Romero said), the Horse Queen of Flax Ranch. Roxanne was quite a woman, Cunningham knew, though he rarely saw her on Flax Ranch. Voyeur, entrepreneur, Roxanne used her ranch as tax shelter, some loss to write off. As if loss could be written off. Roxanne drove a vintage red Cadillac—her chariot—and was usually off hobnobbing at The Groves. She left Fern in charge to maintain a semblance of order and legitimacy. You'll have to ride the horses now dear, she told Fern, after giving old Romero the heave ho. Dip into petty cash and buy yourself an outfit. Fern was well-heeled—Cunningham would give her that.

Good morning, dirty chore boy. Fern's usual salutation.

Hep, Princess, Cunningham's pat reply.

Fern took herself seriously, overdressed trainer to the crop, cap, and new crimson cummerbund. Petite. Small hands and feet, Arabian chin. Lips. Lips you could drink of, Romero claimed. Ach! Don't bother. Cunningham was no butterfly. Alas, no Mexican hummingbird. The fairy tale took a swan dive into the moldering dung heap months ago, and Cunningham no longer dreamt about cultured young princess falling for rumpsprung young hayseed. He still, though, managed a ribald fantasy or twelve. Imagined rolling her in the haymow like Romero did, unbridling and saddle soaping her in the tack room, peeling those delicious licorice riding pants, eating an orange.

As soon fart purple blossoms. As soon crawl into a horse's ear. Cunningham had piled up large the phantasmagoric episodes the summer long, but they were reduced to littleness each time he saw her.

You get started on the boarders, Fern ordered, again as usual, as if Cunningham didn't know his job. Anything I should know? She posed with her crop under her chin. Hitler. Napoleon. A beautiful runt.

Everyone's present and accounted for. A little heat yet in Purple's foreleg. No other injuries to speak of. No miracles or tragedies to write of. Spilling Salvador, Cunningham stood: Ishmael, Quasi Moto. I've saddled Oh's Profit for you.

And that was that. Fern entered Oh's stall, led the handsome three-year-old colt into the aisle and mounted him, pretty as you please. Didn't even need a leg up. She walked down the aisle toward the uneven training track, all buck-oh-five of her, high in the throne, as if she weren't breaking his overgrown heart with every regal step toward daylight. Ta. And a twitch of the crop. Tsss.

The boarder horses were housed under the same roof as the thoroughbreds, and as far off limits to Cunningham as the thoroughbreds themselves. Some were former racers, trained for steeplechase or dressage after they'd lost a step. Each was worth more than Cunningham could earn in ten summers. And besides, what would he do on those tiny saddles and in those tiny stirrups? His big feet and can. The boarders were lined up in a row of twenty stalls, same as the thoroughbreds, and Cunningham's job with the boarders was the same. Water, muck, feed.

In between the racers and the boarders was the riding arena, where the rich women and girls came to take their riding lessons from Princess Fern. Cunningham shuffled though the dark, privileged shavings on the arena floor—Salvador pussyfooting behind—past the tack room with its harnesses, saddles and lithesome bridles hung like torture devices on wooden pegs in the near darkness. Romero's old cot. He emerged into a cacophony of horsey brays and bleatings.

And then it was to work again. Cunningham watered the horses and began the arduous process of leading them out to pasture. There was no reason to separate the boarders, however. Gelded, aged, socialized by socialites, they knew how to get along. They even had windows cut into their stall doors so they could poke their heads through and watch Cunningham at his business. Leading the boarders out was especially painful, though, because each time Cunningham emerged into daylight, he had to watch Fern out there on some stretch of the track and wish it could be him training the young thoroughbreds, sculpting mere ability into that rarest of traits—talent.

There was Fern on the backstretch now, on Purple Moment, riding her too hard, as usual.

Fern was no trainer, though she looked the part. That was Romero's job—until he broke his back. And this was Romero's track. Before Romero, the talented horses on Flax Ranch had to be trained in the city at the racetracks—Balmoral or Arlington—in those efficient Mexican quarters hidden from the grandstands. It was Romero's dream to have his own track here, at home. Train winners. And together Romero and Cunningham built the track, turned the sod with the old disc, dragged it smooth, unloaded yards upon yards of sand, dragged some more, until finally, after a straight two months of sweat broken only by rain delays, it was right.

During that stretch of frantic work, which had to be done in addition to the regular chores—horses jockeyed to temporary paddocks—Romero moved out of his trailer in Shady Valley and into the tack room. They worked on the grounds until dusk settled, and then relaxed in the tack room, just the two of them. It was nice in there. No bulldozer noises permeated the walls. Cunningham and Romero would smoke and talk by candlelight in the near dark, the tack harmless as decoration. Romero would speak of the old days, breaking horses in Mexico with his *padre*, and Cunningham would fold his large body on the floor next to Romero's cot, happily nostalgic, as if in love.

Afterward, he rode his bicycle home in the cricketed, tree-frogged darkness, and the trip between the two ends of Blood's Point Road felt like no distance at all.

But Romero's own dream was his undoing, last spring on the muddy track, when Nonnie Nellie spooked, slipped, fell, and birdlike Romero was crushed under the weight of her. An ambulance blared and beamed onto Flax Ranch, startling the horses.

Every horseman breaks his back at least once, Romero said, prone in his hospital bed. Not to worry. My father broke his back. *Mi tio* broke his twice, didn't stop him. A broken back is not anything. I have broke my arms, a leg, *muchos* ribs. My nose broke five times and look at here, still *guapo, no*? Romero, plastered, was released from the hospital on strict orders. He went back to Mexico to convalesce, but returned with fused vertebrae and permanent nerve damage, unable to ride again.

And then came the quick descent. Romero put himself out to pasture. He strapped on the nose bag and grew himself a paunch. Talked about all the losses one had to endure, how they piled up over the years. He paid no attention to Fern or Roxanne, and that, more than anything, Cunningham believed, is what cost him his job. Romero always said how that tandem needed more grooming and exercise than the horses. It was how he had maintained his fighting weight.

The Mexican trainer turned bitter before he was sent packing. Evenings in the cluttered tack room Romero spoke poison. Do you know what the inside of a woman feels like, *gordo*? It has teeth, take it from Romero. And fuck horses. *Putas negras. Caballos estan putas tontas.* Fuck horses and toothy women, *hijo.* You're lucky to be *feo y fuerte y tonto y lento y gordo y... y... y....* Romero waved his crop, some wand. *Soy Romero, El Desecho.* The wasted. You have an easy life, *hijo.* A good back is all you need. But you'll break it one day. A big horse, *el caballo muy grande,* will knock you down and step on you, and step on you again. Go back to cows, *hijo*, slow and fat like you.

Cunningham looked down and saw then that Romero's pants were wet. The trainer looked down too, and then their eyes met. I piss where I lie, he said. This is my sty. Here is how you muck it.

Cunningham left the tack room. He made the long ride back to his coop, pedaling slowly, steering crookedly. A moon lit the early night: dying violet. On the horizon loomed what could be taken for a cloud bank. Cunningham squinted and saw the cloud bank materialize into a solid wall of gray houses. Slowly and steadily the storm front crept toward Cunningham and his pitiful little life. Head down, Cunningham pedaled hard now. He wanted to beat the storm. Legs like pistons, his pedals turned the chain around the sprocket—turned the wheels over the gravel—until, by-and-by, the grist of space was ground. Cunningham was home, call it that, where he could forget about the rumbling bulldozers, the ugly gray houses that fenced his pasture, threatened to close the curtain on his horizon.

But the stable boy festered there, unable to sleep on his own skinny roost. Unable to crush want. He closed his eyes then and willed: *Crush Want. Crush Want. Crush Want.* No good. Cunningham heard bats flying around. Was this what life was all about, as Romero said, a string of losses? That first loss came when you yanked the colt from its mother's tit. From then on, a downhill slide toward shitsville—each loss worse than the last, until the big crapola left you sitting helpless in your own piss. That's what happened to his old man, after all, and his ma suffered her part. The old man was probably sitting in his own piss now, bad legs wrapped around some bar stool in Bergamot, USA. And here was Cunningham, well on his way, sitting in the chicken shit. What could you do about it? If he was smaller he could race horses. At least have the illusion of winning before the grand crapola. But Cunningham was no thoroughbred. No boarder horse, even. In his puny imagination he was unable to conjure any winning ride or cram his big ass into some horse's ear, unable to fly the coop even with his eyes tight shut.

A sleepless night, a tired ride to work, a moldering shit pile in the fogged-in pasture, the tack room: empty. Some white feline haunting his shadow. Cunningham mucked and tugged and carted, and after he was tired, he mucked some more.

The pain was immediate. He felt it before he knew what was happening. Shot in the back maybe, or stabbed with a spud fork. Some bastard had plugged him good. Damn. Then he snapped to. One of the boarders had reached out and taken a bite of him, right between the shoulder blades. Fucking horse. He ripped off his T-shirt and danced in pain. Salvador crouched, making himself smaller. Cunningham ran for daylight, plunged his shirt into the horse trough and slapped the wet mop onto his throbbing back. Doubled over, he opened his eyes: blurry, then focused. There was a robin red breast on the damp ground before him. He focused on the robin. The pain. The robin.

The redbreast had hold of a night crawler and was tugging the worm from its hole. Her feet firmly planted, her pretty feathers ruffling, she was making ground on the stubborn worm, backing up and redoubling her grip. So vicious for a little bird. She shook her head like a killer, some dog got hold of a snake. Just then, the long worm stretched taut and broke, sending the robin backward, her beak full of worm-half. But she wasn't happy with just half and darted quickly back to the hole. The worm's bottom half, disconnected from its head, gave easily. The robin tilted her head back and slid the worm half down her throat in an easy gulp. Then she hopped back to the fatter head, made short work of it too.

There was a white blur, Salvador pouncing. Too slow, fat cat. The robin flapped off and Salvador looked at Cunningham stupidly. It's OK cat, nice try. Everything seemed to calm, and Cunningham's pain spread out, then relaxed. He stood up. Out of the corner of his eye, he caught Fern flagging him. On Purple Moment. She was prancing back to the thoroughbred door, but Purple Moment was giving her trouble. She was skittering sideways toward the door, prancing and half-bucking. Fern was holding on and hollering to Cunningham to get his ass over there.

Cunningham lumbered over the fence and met Fern just inside the barn door. Take reins, Fern sang out. Something's gotten into this bitch. Cunningham took the reins and Fern slipped off, safely, luckily, just as Purple Moment reared back, yanking the reins from Cunningham's grip, cutting his palms. Ouch. Goddamn. Goddamn that hurts.

Get out of the way, Fern ordered. She was sweating at the brow and her cute little riding cap was half-cocked, loosening her blond hair. Fern grabbed the reins, but Purple Moment was still wired. The horse reared again, pulling Fern with her. Stand, you bitch, she shouted, brandishing the crop. Fucking stand, hear me. She lashed out with the crop and caught Purple Moment across the muzzle. Again. There was immense heat coming from the big animal, as if it might combust.

Suddenly, a white blur. Salvador, *gato loco*, lept from the shadows. The cat bounded from straw bale to stall wall to horse's back. Cunningham had seen how the cats at the racetrack stables would climb on the horses' backs and curl there, relaxing the antsy beasts, themselves sleeping in that sweet spot between rump and withers, a mutual lullaby.

But Salvador had other things in mind. He was atop the horse, digging in. The world's tiniest jockey: Salvador The Small But Mighty. Purple Moment would have none of it. She reared back then, and over. Fern fell backward on her ass and Salvador leapt easily away, landing safely on all fours. The big bay horse came down with a resounding crash, her head impacting the stall wall. She heaved, trying to stand, but flopped over unable, her head striking wood again with a hollow thud. She twitched then, and sighed like you do when it's all she wrote.

Purple Moment's soft brown eyes rolled. The thunderheads in them thinned to cirrus, then blanched. She was still. Her body, still hot, seemed to fill the air of the thin corridor. Some horse whinnied. Salvador licked a dirty paw.

I think I killed the bitch, Fern said, shaking. She was all undone, everything loose that was tight before. That will teach her. She's dead now and she deserved it. Fucking cat's the one who did it.

Cunningham, sore in the hands and back, went to the horse and leaned over her. He was sweating, driplets falling from his big nose and forehead onto Purple Moment's massive flanks, mixing with her own pearl lather and dark wetness. He stroked her face and beautiful, feathered ears.

Cunningham! Cunningham, your back's bleeding, Fern called, still sitting in the dirt. Cunningham, you've been bitten.

The stable boy was still draped over the horse. She ain't dead, he said, just knocked south of plumb. That was a beautiful piece of work. A maiden-breaker all the way around.

Cunningham watched as Purple Moment's eyes made a slow revolution in her skull. The storm clouds gathered, gained a positive momentum. She was coming round the backstretch, eating up ground. Good odds the big crapola was still a ways off, on some other stretch of track. That race would conclude in its own good time. This, on the other hand, was a second wind, Cunningham was sure of it. Best celebrate the victories when they come. Yes, she'd eke out a winner on this one for sure. Purple Moment, by a nose.

About Town

The public debt will not be paid this year. The same will happen with many private debts. There will be many eclipses of male and female virtue this year, some visible, and some invisible.

—*The Farmers Almanac*, 1800

Shady Valley Days

Town

Dale's kid brother Connie would remember it as square and flat, not like a valley at all, more like a vast plain. One two-lane highway skewered the town, cutting in on the south and exiting on the north. In town the highway was called Main Street and outside of town the highway was simply called the Blacktop. If you drove into town either way you saw posted an official Wisconsin State Highway sign that read:

Shady Valley
Pop. 1,000

And although the population had drained to nearer 850 than 1,000, nobody wanted to see that sign changed. After all, 1,000 was a nice round number, surely more respectable than 850, and more easily divisible anyway.

Aside from taverns and churches, of which there were several, Shady Valley had exactly one of everything: one river which bisected the town perpendicular to Main Street; one school where students entered from the south when they were five or six and exited from the north when they were eighteen or twenty; one lumber mill, one grain elevator, one trailer court; one laundry, one library, one grocery; one park, one bank, one gas stop; one five and dime, one greasy spoon, one shithole Hilton Hotel even, and most recently, one almost-empty pizzeria. Of churches there were two, a First Methodist and a First Lutheran, and of taverns three, a First Farmer's Inn and a Second Farmer's Inn—called respectively the South End and the North End to avoid confusion—and another in the middle, an old brick affair with a false front called the Wooden Nickel.

Shady Valley was ten blocks long and ten blocks wide, and even though Joseph Smith had steered his people well clear of Shady Valley en route to the promised land, North End publican Clifford Duncan had half the town convinced a small band of Mormons had laid down the original street plan. "It had to be the Mormons," Clifford said. "This is the squarest town in Wisconsin." Just two roads leaked out the back end of town. Blood's Point, running out past the trailer court, was a dead end. The Blacktop led out past Shady Valley Quarry to Bergamot, another little town about as easy to figure as Shady Valley but far enough away, until lately, so no one had to bother.

Second Farmer's

In the days before Dale Grim made his big jump off Grim Ledge into Glory Hole at the quarry, Clifford Duncan sat as usual on the wrong side of his nice lacquered bar playing out his role as Shady Valley's Chief Detractor to a couple of boys just clocked out of Jake's Lumber Mill and anyone else who would listen.

No farmers came to Clifford Duncan's North End, they all went to the South End, which was the First Farmer's. Clifford thought it would be a good joke to name his bar Second Farmer's but the real farmers held no truck with such folderol. Most of Clifford's clientele were has-beens bucked out of some other small town or local flunkies who either dropped out of Shady Valley High or graduated but never managed to move away. This is not to say that there were no successful or upright citizens in Shady Valley, just that they didn't often see their way into Clifford's place. Still, his bar was considerably more lucrative than the South End, though not through any talent of Clifford's. The North End featured a drive-up liquor window in the back where local kids could pull in at night in their rusted-out Chevy Novas and three-quarter-ton GMCs and buy a case of Budweiser, a pack of weeds and a fifth of Night Train for the road. Clifford's wife Roberta, who kept the books, liked to say that the back end of Second Farmer's was the business end and the long lacquered bar top in front was just for show.

Clifford had been in town only a few years—having moved from the Milwaukee suburbs—and he preferred the term publican to a barkeep. He liked to say that Shady Valley was a nothing town with nobody in it, and most everyone sitting at his bar had grown enough ashamed of themselves to believe him. Anyway, they figured if they argued much with Clifford Duncan they were just liable to prove him right.

The Next Walt Hriniak

Dickie Flynn, who at twenty-two already ran the big saw at Jake's Lumber Mill, had heard about enough of Clifford Duncan for one night. Dickie didn't like Clifford, but he had the cheapest tap beer in town, and you couldn't argue with cheap. He tried again to remind Clifford of Shady Valley's most famous alum. "What about Hriniak?" Dickie said. He was speaking of Walt Hriniak, all-state two sports in '69, who went on to homer in his very first major league at bat with the Detroit Tigers. "That's somebody," Dickie said.

"Walt Hriniak's a bum," said Clifford. "I know Walt Hriniak. He hit a home run in his first at bat sure, but how many did he have after that? Sixteen? Big Deal. You show me a worse bum whose whole life amounted to sixteen home runs." Clifford tipped his empty beer mug at Roberta, back manning the till. "That Hriniak couldn't hit a curve ball to save his eggs. And what's he do now?

Dickie sat up straight on his stool. "He's got his own business in Milwaukee."

"Oh, yeah," Clifford said. "I seen him at 5th and Burleigh driving a meat truck. Big Deal. Heap big Shady Valley star sells meatballs in the ghetto."

Dickie didn't argue further. He didn't know where 5th and Burleigh was. And he didn't know how many home runs Walt Hriniak had in total, only that he dinged one his very first up, which seemed like something. When Dickie was in high school Coach always said how Walt was some kind of a hero. The last time Shady Valley made state in football was '69, Walt's year. "Any of you could be the Next Walt Hriniak," Coach said, though everybody knew Dale Grim was the only true Next Walt Hriniak material. Now Clifford made Hriniak seem like a nobody, which made Dickie's friend Dale seem like nobody too. Dale was due home next week and Dickie wouldn't have Clifford Duncan disrespecting him.

Fat Clifford sat like an old jukebox begging to be plugged. How come Clifford was such a bigshot selling beer and pretzels? Dickie looked around for help. Hoody Roach was with him, but not really with him. He eyeballed his beer like he'd weld a bead on it. There was Roberta busy at the till. She was a good-looking woman, and she paid the bills. How did that slob Clifford get a woman like Roberta, and why the hell did she put up with him?

Dickie decided to take one more poke. "What about Grim?" he said.

"Grim can get in line with Hriniak," Clifford said.

"Exactly," Dickie said.

Connie Grim

Connie hadn't seen his brother in a long time, but now Dale was coming home again on furlough. Connie was only six when Dale left the first time. Now he was eight. He remembered Dale heading off with the big green bag. Then it seemed like all anybody did was wait. "Wait till your brother gets home on furlough," his mother said.

Then Dale came home again with the big green bag, and nobody had to wait any longer.

But Dale wasn't around much when he was home. "Everybody needs a little piece of him while he's here," his mother said. She seemed happy. Then Dale left again and she said to wait.

While Connie waited he remembered Dale—one time standing in front of the basement mirror shaving and another time riding his black snowmobile hellbent in the green grass. He was crazy. Connie remembered Dale's bicep and how it was cut through the middle by a rope from the Marines. Connie asked Dale to make a muscle, and when Dale made a muscle with his cut bicep the muscle made not one bulge but two large bulges.

Connie thought a lot about Dale. He even made a list of the best memories about Dale so he wouldn't forget them. The best memory had to be riding on the back of Dale's yellow dirt bike. Connie remembered riding the yellow motorcycle out of the gravel drive. They lived on Blood's Point Road past Flax Ranch and the road was long and dusty. They went to town and made a turn, went a long way down the Blacktop and made another turn, over a bridge, over another bridge. The ride went on like that, the motorcycle speeding up with a high-pitched whine and then slowing down with a sputtering cough. Connie held on tight. He could feel the heat of the muffler on the insides of his legs but he kept his legs away from the muffler like he was told.

Later, they made it back to town, but from the other direction! They stopped for gas and Connie got off. He looked down Main Street both ways, first the way they had gone, then the way they came back. He asked Dale how he did that. Dale gave him a strange look and said, "We went around the block, Dipshit."

These were the exact words Connie remembered. He remembered very clearly the disbelieving look in Dale's eyes and that his brother had called him Dipshit.

Mary Loomis

If self-absorbed, at least frequent and full of passionate desperation at first, then pleasurably steady if predictable for a number of months, but gradually diminishing in style and stamina and finally petering out altogether except for an excited flourish once in a blue moon. That's how the letters went. No, she hadn't been good, but San Diego, California was like, what, a thousand miles away?

And don't tell her it was just Dale and the other brawny privates on that Tijuana weekend after he finally finished Basic.

"You've never seen anything like the ocean," Dale had written. "You wouldn't believe the blue."

Yes, Mary would believe it. She'd ogled Dale's blue eyes often enough. And she and Dale had been swimming in Blue Hole at the quarry dozens of times. They'd made love in the blue water and on the rocks looking out over the blue water. Had Dale forgotten where he came from? "Look," she finally wrote back. "Don't fill my head full of too many pretty pictures. The ocean is a long ways from Shady Valley, USA."

Mary got sick of waiting. That's what it came down to, finally. She had done all right the first year, writing more letters than she got and waiting for furlough. Did she love him? You bet, and didn't she prove it to him when he came home on furlough? But with Dale you had to be hard or he took advantage. You had to look out for yourself first. Dale's problem was that he was too beautiful, and beautiful boys had a bad habit of looking over your shoulder all the while.

Sure, Dale was always the golden boy. She knew what she had signed up for. But while he was away, he seemed to grow more golden while everyone else just grew, well, tired of waiting. And people in town still called her Dale's Mary! Her own mother told her to sit tight. "It's not like your ovaries are going to shrivel up, honey," she said. "Christ, you got time."

But Mary was done waiting. She wrote Dale her last letter telling him so. She put down exactly what she felt in the letter, but when she read it over, she was confused about what she had written. Still, she sent the letter. The last sentence read, "You're not around here to get dirty like the rest of us, Dale."

That was six months ago. Now Mary felt a little bad. Dale had gotten dirty, evidently. He was coming home for good this time. He had beaten that Minnesota boy badly enough to be discharged. Golden boy was coming home tarnished and now what? Would she be there to meet him? Sure as rain. But he better not expect much sympathy from Mary Loomis.

Bergamot Joe's

When Dickie got sick of the lunchtime fish fries or burger baskets at the Wooden Nickel, he came down to Joe's Pizza for a pepperoni slice. Joe's had been open two years but was almost always empty. People in town called the place Bergamot Joe's from the start, on account of Joe hailed from Bergamot, and he opened his first pizzeria there. It might be true that everyone likes a good pizza, but no place called Bergamot Joe's was going to thrive in Shady Valley, USA. If they felt like pizza, folks would as soon drive to Bergamot Joe's in Bergamot as step foot in Bergamot Joe's on Main Street, Shady Valley.

Still, it was quiet in Joe's and they had a decent slice. Today, Dickie mostly wanted for quiet. He sat in the orange booth by the big picture window and took three letters from his pocket. It was true that Dale was coming home. Dickie got the letter just last week. This was only the second letter Dale had sent him from the Marines. Dickie reflected that besides birthday cards from aunts and things, these were the only two real letters he had ever gotten in the mail. The first Dale had sent when he was still in Basic two years ago. That first letter was a good one, and Dickie had saved it after showing it around. This second letter was just two paragraphs long. It announced

Dale's coming home and ended with the statement, "This ain't for no furlough."

Before this, Dickie had his own letter written and ready to send. In the letter he wrote about how he hoped finally to move out of the trailer court. There was a little house on 3rd Street he had his eye on, the old Petrowski place. He had been saving and saving, and he couldn't wait to break the good news to somebody. Now, rereading Dale's newest letter and his own, Dickie realized he couldn't send the letter he had written.

Dickie looked up. Judy Homer, the pastor from First Lutheran, stood outside the window looking in. She motioned to the empty seat across from Dickie. Dickie looked around. No one else was in the restaurant. He looked back at the pastor outside the window and shrugged. The pastor walked around the building and into the empty room.

"I wonder if I might have a few moments of your time, Mr. Flynn," the pastor said. Just then, Dickie's pizza came. He couldn't very well say he was leaving.

"All right," Dickie said. "Just a minute though." He got up, gathering the letters. In the bathroom, he crumpled two letters and dropped them into the wire basket by the pisser. The two-year-old letter from Dale he refolded neatly into his wallet.

Love From Dale

Hey Dickie,

I'm sending this to you, but it's meant for you and Hoods. (You may have to read it to him, ha ha.) Anyway, you wouldn't believe where I am. In the infirmary! I'll be here for a couple of weeks, and then I have to go back and do my last week of Basic. Basic is some grueling shit. Think first day of pads, triple sessions in the heat. Guys were puking every day, and then getting their asses kicked behind the barracks for slowing us up. Tell you the truth I'm grateful to be out of commission for a while. I didn't think I was gonna make it.

Anyway, I fucked up my arm pretty bad. Long story short, this Minnesota puke behind me during rope drills climbed up my ass and knocked me off. I fell about twenty feet. The rope caught me, but I had it wrapped around my arm. I was just hanging there. Drill Sergeant had to climb up and cut me down, but the rope severed my bicep. The whole thing's in a cast now and will be for another two weeks. We'll see how I come out of it. Tell you one thing, the asshole who made me fall, I'll teach him where Peter buys his beer.

Enough about me. How's things at home? You ought to sign up for classes at Tech, Dickie. Seriously. You're smart enough. I'm not too smart or I wouldn't be here, I guess. People asked me why the Marines. I don't know. Those two years at State, I guess. I proved I wasn't College Material, but you are, Dickie. (You too, Hoods.) I'm good at sports, sure, but that's because I'm good at taking orders. Someone's on my back telling me what to do and how to do it I'm fine. Otherwise I'm hopeless. You know what I mean.

Who knows, maybe four years here will teach me something, and then I can try again. For right now, I'm nobody, and I can handle that here. I can't handle it in Shady.

Anyway, I'm signing off. Say hey to Mary for me. Take her out swimming some time to the quarry like she likes. I'd rather she go out with you than someone else. (but keep your hands off her—you too, Hoods.) She's sore at me for leaving, but she still writes. Says, get this, "You can be replaced." Man, she busts my balls. I guess I'm pretty lucky for her, though.

Let's see, what else. Stay the hell away from the North End too, why don't you. Mary said you guys practically live there.

That Clifford Duncan's poison. Doesn't have anything good to say about anybody. You know he keeps people down just to keep his fat ass up. Shady Valley's full of cats like that. Tell you another thing, though, old Shady doesn't look too bad from where I'm sitting. I know you're supposed to say out loud it's a shithole and you can't wait to leave, but that's a helluva note. (Now I'm starting to talk like my old man!) Anyway, no sense living your whole life ashamed of where you come from.

Ha. Listen to me, like I know whether to shit or go blind. That's enough of that. Will write again soon. Check in on my folks and kid bro for me. Sorry to leave the little shave come up by himself, but we all had to.

No semper fi shit, just peace,

Grim

One Elevator

Stanley Booker stood at the edge of the corn watching the last hole of his gravel quarry fill up green. These were his two Shady Valley investments, grain and gravel. His days in the gravel business were over now, but no matter. Everywhere he looked, Stanley saw green.

'Knee high by the Fourth of July' went the saying, and here it was June twentieth and the corn was chest high, chin high! It was a hot, wet season and the corn was growing like smartweed. Grain prices were falling steady and Stanley had appointments through the week. The problem with these farmers is that their memories were too short. Four years of decent prices for corn and beans and all the buzz at the tavern was about a new era in large grains. The whole countryside went up in corn and beans. Now, a bumper crop was on the way, and Stanley was set to make a killing. He owned the only elevator in town. Either farmers came to him and paid his price, or they took their lumps in the glut market. These farmers, here they had a perfect growing season, and they'd have to harvest three bushels to make two.

Stanley Booker had bigger fish to fry. He was the lone visionary in a town of purblind peasants. If there was a new era, it wasn't in large grains. Here the population of Shady Valley was leaking away, and Stanley held the golden plug. Thirteen miles of good blacktop linked Shady Valley and Bergamot, and Stanley stood smack in the middle, on prime development land.

Consolidation was the only answer to Shady Valley woes. Hell, the high school couldn't even field a football team, and Bergamot had the same problem over there. This big mouth woman pastor and this has-been local council were too dim to see it, but they would have to see it. Stanley saw it now. These would be prime estates, lake properties like at Bergamot Pond but overlooking clear water! His quarry was only fifty miles from Madison by good roads. The city was expanding, boy, make no mistake. Folks in the capital wanted small town values—if only on the weekends—and they wanted a big house with a view. Stanley had just the recipe. He'd slope down that south wall and build a beach. Fill this green hole with speckled trout. These high cliffs would be done up in two-story houses with cedar fence for safety.

Stanley looked down from the high cliff to the emerald pool. His knees got a little weak from the distance. He had best post the property soon. It wouldn't keep the hooligans out, but it would save liability. One of them might be just stupid enough to jump. The hooligans had already claimed that other hole. They called it Blue Hole. Stanley came down to chase them out once in a while. He came on hot days when there was more flesh exposed. They had delicious flesh, some of these hooligans, and Stanley had got himself some good shows.

They had probably found this new green hole by now, Stanley guessed. He'd best get his property posted.

First Farmer's

Later that week, Dickie and Hoody decided to try the South End for dollar night. It felt nice to sit up at the bar and drink nice cold two-dollar beers at a dollar each. The scenery was a little different too. The bartop at the South End was a square with the bartender in the middle. This meant that instead of looking at yourself in the mirror behind the bar, you looked across at other people sitting at the bar. Dickie didn't like this so much. He guessed he'd rather look at himself young than look at himself old.

Tonight the scenery wasn't so great. It seemed like the whole North End crowd had shifted south. Where were the farmers in their green and red seed caps talking about the weather and the price per bushel? Dickie used to make fun of that small talk, but now it didn't seem so small. He liked it better than all the big talk at the North End. Maybe he and Hoody would have to spend their dollars down here for a while. But there weren't any farmers tonight. Corn growing like weeds, there ought to more farmers in here to celebrate.

Dickie nudged Hoody Roach on the stool next to him, but Hoody didn't budge. Fucking Hoody. He was checked out again. He'd better get his act together. Dickie got Hoody the job driving the flatbed for Jake's, but he wasn't sure how long he'd keep the job. Half the time he was off in neverland.

Hoody had a lipful of Copenhagen and half a cupful of black spit next to his beer. It looked to Dickie like he was trying to decide which one to drink.

"Pick your poison," Dickie said. "I've had a enough of this place." He finished his beer in a big gulp and walked out. It was a hot night. Too hot to walk all the way to the North End. He might just as well have a nightcap at the Wooden Nickel.

Hoody Roach

Hoody was thinking about Mary Loomis and her necklace of bruises. Who had gotten there first? Last night he had taken Mary out to Glory Hole in his Cutlass. At first, he'd just taken her out there swimming like Dale said, but who was Dale kidding? Mary had a mind of her own. He parked the Cutlass where they could see the water filling in the new green hole. Mary had said the color was glorious. She's the one who started the raunchy jokes by naming it Glory Hole.

It was a warm night. They stretched out on the warm hood of the Cutlass. A little batch of stars reflected in the glassy quarry, some bright, some dim. Mary said Dale was coming home, and it wasn't for no furlough. They both worried for a little while. Then Hoody found a joint in his shirt pocket. It would be all right. They passed the joint and lay quiet on their backs, listening to the Cutlass tick out the last of its heat.

Hoody didn't mention the bruises. He was afraid if he upset her she might ask to go. He leaned to kiss her neck where someone else had put the bruises. Mary stayed put. He kissed her neck and pulled at the white shirt tucked neatly into her jeans. Mary was tense. All this talk of Dale she might not want to. But the white shirt came easily after all. Her stomach was flat and bare and dark against the white shirt. Even in the dark he could see how tan. God, Hoody thought.

Mary looked up at him with her big eyes and then looked away, giving Hoody her bruised neck. Her mouth was just open and Hoody saw the white kernels of her teeth. Far off on the Blacktop a car passed dragging its muffler. Mary laughed.

"What are you laughing at?" Hoody said.

Mary said, "Shhhhh."

Hoody put his hand on the flat of her bare stomach and left it there awhile. Finally Mary breathed in, opening a beautiful little gap between her stomach and her jeans. Hoody slid his hand into her jeans. He felt first a ridge of silk and then a heat like he had never felt before.

Hoody was back at the bar. He looked down. He had squeezed the handle of his beer mug so hard that it snapped. He held the glass handle yet, but his beer was spilled. His thumb was bleeding.

Hoody paid, banged out of the bar and out onto Main Street. God, it was fucking hot. He stood under the neon Farmer's Inn sign and saw the hulking black figure of the grain elevator there at the edge of town. The other way twin rows of dull yellow street lights lit Main Street all the way down. After that it was dark. Hoody walked for the North End watching his shadow grow and shrink between the street lights.

Dickie wasn't there. Hoody ordered a double granddad. He sat at the bar and sucked the cut place between his thumb and finger. It was final, Hoody thought. Mary was fucking Dickie too.

The bar was almost empty. Clifford sat heaped onto his stool. Behind the bar, Roberta was scrubbing something. Clifford so much as opened his fat yap, Hoody would kill him.

But the bar was quiet. Outside on Main Street a car passed, dragging its muffler. Finally, Hoody got up.

"You want my opinion?" Clifford said after Hoody walked out.

"No," Roberta said. "I don't want your opinion."

Love from Dickie

Hey Grim,

I don't even know if you'll get this in time, but here goes anyway. I had a long mushy love letter for you, but then after your last note, I thought I better cut mine down. I'm over at the Wooden Nickel now writing at the bar. (One Nut's looking at me funny.) Anyway, it's good to hear you're coming home. Everybody here wants to see you. I'm sorry to hear about the discharge. I know that Minnesota kid had it coming. Don't worry, I haven't said anything to anyone. Nobody knows.

Let's see, news. You know how it goes around here. Not much happens very fast. You probably heard Booker and some of the bigshots in town are talking about consolidating with Bergamot. We might not even field a football team this year. It's pitiful to see. Enrollment is too low, I guess. Man, and those kids look like junior high kids. They keep getting smaller and smaller.

That woman pastor and some of the teachers don't want to consolidate. They started a booster club which I might join just for the hell of it. Turns out this booster club cooked up an idea for a weekend fair over the 4th called "Shady Valley Days." Clifford Duncan about shit a cupcake when he heard that. "There ain't enough Shady Valley to fill up one day," he said. Anyway, they're trying to spruce up town to get ready. Out by the population marker they put up a new sign. Says, get this:

Shady Valley
Home of the Detroit Tigers'
~~Walt Hriniak~~

I guess the Tigers hired Hriniak on as third base coach. Somebody already crossed out Hriniak's name, so now it looks like Shady Valley is the home of the Detroit Tigers. That might pack 'em in for Shady Valley Days.

That's about all the town gossip, I guess. It's been hot and wet here. Corn's up to my neck and tasseled out already. Might be a record harvest. It's been so humid we've been working 5:00 until 2:00 shifts at the mill. The saw blades rust overnight on account of the humidity. Even the hay crews around here are knocking off at noon. Everybody's been up to the quarry or in the bar to stay cool. There's a new hole out to the quarry that's got pure green water—bright green, not pisswater green. There's a high cliff, but nobody's jumped yet. The hole's still filling up. Anyway, we'll go out when you get back. Probably not much after you seen the ocean, but it's big news here.

Your folks are fine. Connie's getting big. Your ma said the little shave got kicked off the bus the last week of school for fixing some kid's wagon. Eight years old! She figures he didn't lick it off the grass. Mary's fine too, brown as a nut from laying around waiting for you, I guess. I don't think she's seeing anybody regular. If she is, she doesn't tell me.

Hoody's not so good. Maybe you can talk to him when you get here, see if anybody's home. He's starting to worry people. I left him crapped out on his stool at the South End tonight, in fact.

Well, I gotta go. They're playing a sad song on the juke box. It's called "Last Call."

Everybody here loves you.

Flynn

Shit Hole

Hoody climbed up the stairs to his room at the Hilton. His apartment was the cheapest in the building, what the asshole manager called an efficiency. When Dickie and Mary came over they joked that it was an efficiency because you could cook, fuck and piss and never leave the bed. Now, Hoody fell into bed. Lying on his back, he reached out and ashed his cigarette into the wet sink. The little room began to spin. Hoody liked this spinning and often swallowed a last double at bartime so the room would spin more. Dickie had told him he was crazy. "If the room starts to spin I head for the toilet," Dickie said. Not Hoody. The room could spin all night. It was spinning now, and he let it spin.

He thought about Dale. Hoody had been Dale's backfield partner in high school. When they were seniors, Dale made all-conference, scored twenty-three touchdowns and led Shady Valley to State for just the second time. That year, Hoody had eleven carries for minus-one yard. Coach gave him a token carry each game, but everybody knew Hoody's job was to block for Dale. "Grim is a genius with the football in his hands and a little daylight," Coach told him. "You make daylight for our genius."

Each time Hoody Roach flung his body into the line it was for the team, sure, but more directly it was for Dale, hitting the hole behind him. Hoody never got to see the genius in action, though. If Dale sprung one, chances are Hoody's face would be in the mud. Still, Hoody didn't mind his role. He understood it. After all, Dale was fast and he was slow. Hoody had a hard head, though, and he was strong as a horse. Sometimes in short yards, he could feel Dale's hand on his back, pushing for daylight. Twice that year they hit the end zone that way, standing up. Hoody never scored a touchdown himself, but plowing through the hole ahead of Dale felt as good as sex, or a spinning room.

The team only lost one game that year—to sucking Bergamot no less—and in that game Dale got his bell rung after Hoody missed a block. Coach grabbed him by the face mask and jerked him to the bench. He slapped his helmet. "You listen to me," he said. "Where Grim goes, you go first. That's the only thing you need to think. Ever. Got it? First Roach, then Grim."

Hoody didn't look up. Dale was done for the game. He heard the assistant coach over on the bench asking him a series of questions, What month? How many fingers? Luckily, Shady Valley went on to win the conference ahead of Bergamot, so the players could later joke about that moment. "First Roach, then Grim," his teammates chanted, everywhere they went.

The room was still spinning. Hoody wasn't sleepy anymore. The memories had somehow made him awake. Main Street lit his room dull yellow. Some bugs buzzed in the window. He could see everything from the bed: the sink, the toilet. He mashed his cigarette in the sink. The hot ash hissed in the wet sink. For the first time in a long time, Hoody thought very clearly. It came down to this. Living now was shit compared to living then.

Glory Hole

Dale would have to jump. Sun-kissed bodies dangled from the lower edges of the quarry and floated in the green water waiting. Dale first said he would jump simply because it felt good to be home and find something new. New water filled the quarry, water as green and pure as Dickie's promise. The cliff above was so steep and sheer that there was no question he could jump. But he made the decision from below, swimming in the cool water and looking up at the sheer cliff. "I can jump it," he said to no one in particular, and his friends laughed at first. He laughed at first too.

Then Hoody Roach said, "Grim's gonna jump," and the sound carried over the water and bounced between the rock walls.

Now, Dale stood bare to the waist above the quarry on the high cliff. He wore his yellow sneakers to protect his feet. The water looked like a shallow pond from here. And the sheer cliff looked not sheer at all but slanted outward toward the water. Dale was no cliff diver. Even jumping off the thirty-foot cliff into Blue Hole had purpled his arms and crushed out his breath when he didn't hit the water right. This new cliff was eighty feet. They'd measured by letting a length of rope down from the cliff.

But here he was on the edge and everyone was watching: his old friends from Shady Valley High, pukes from Bergamot High, and some older ones who graduated and grew beards but never moved away, like Boney Heller and his bad gang. Mary was down there with Carmen Purifoy and some other girls, soaking their toes in the green water. They all hung around waiting. For them, Dale would have to jump. How much of his life had been like that? It was the same with the Minnesota kid. Dale had told a couple of grunts he would get even, and then his statement seemed to grow bigger than he was. The whole platoon seemed to demand he follow through. His arm had healed, he didn't even want to beat the kid anymore. It was like he was pushed.

But it had always been that way. Dale had never done a thing on his own. There was a level platform anyway, so fuck it, he could hit the edge running. He counted off twelve long strides backward from the edge, as far as he could go, to where the wall of corn grew thick and green above his head. The corn was massive. Spun blonde tassels spilled from its ears. Dickie Flynn and Hoody Roach stood there by the corn.

Dickie said it was enough. "All right, the show's over," he said. "You're not jumping." Hoody was silent. Dickie gripped Dale's arm where it had been hurt, but there was no real force in his grip. Dale stared at the edge. For a while it was just the three of them. Dale couldn't see the others spread out on the lower cliff edges and in the water. Still, they were there.

Dale broke his friend's grip and ran from the corn. By the time he hit the edge of the cliff he had hit his stride. He planted his left foot just at the edge and propelled himself out. His launch was a good one, a near-perfect launch. He was flying then, feet first, his body arcing outward and downward. The wind rushed by like a rush of cheers and the water moved closer, but slowly. He let out two long, full yells and felt like he was free.

Then Dale felt his injured arm where the rope seemed to hold it still. As if hanging from the rope, his body swung full force back in toward the cliff.

First Lutheran

"In search of comfort, I rummaged through my husband's tools and brought out his measuring tape. I had often watched my husband potter about, measuring this and measuring that. It seemed a strange but tranquil endeavor. It looked comforting, his measuring.

"At first I walked about the house and measured all manner of small things: a tooth brush, one of Peter's loafers, that poor lone fish he has stuffed over the mantle—the mantle itself, its length and width. I measured several things before I realized I was practicing for something bigger, learning to read all those tiny gradations—the ultimate difference between an eighth and a sixteenth. Then I measured live things, the length of my own arms. I measured Peter's girth and wingspan, the length of his embrace. I bade our son stand against the kitchen door frame with his shoes off and chin up and marked his height in the wood grain. Then I bade Peter and Christopher lie down on the living room floor so I could measure the length of my son and husband together. When Peter looked skeptical, I said not to worry. He could think of it as a math lesson for Christopher. Peter seemed to accept this. I made the measuring tape walk as Peter said I could do.

"Unaccountably, I wanted to measure still bigger things. I took out Peter's ladder and climbed up on the roof. Peter said I was becoming a little ridiculous, but Christopher seemed amazed to watch his mother climb a ladder and make the measuring tape walk. I measured the length of the roof along the gutter and then the width from peak to gutter. I measured Christopher's little dormer, and then I climbed to the edge of the peak. Holding just the silver tab, I let the heavy yellow part of the tape slide pleasurably down to the ground, and then I drew it up again, as one draws water from a well.

"By this time I realized that yes, the act of measuring was indeed tranquil and comforting, somehow meaningful. But standing up there on the peak I realized that I had a larger question in mind. I became curious about where I might measure the highest point in Shady Valley. This seemed important. After all, I had been a citizen of this town for nine years. I had a right to know. And so, permitting myself Peter's assistance, I set myself the task.

"Now, I come before for you on this Sabbath, humbly, and before the Lord, to give my testament.

"The congregation might take some pride in knowing that the steeple of its own First Lutheran Church is a sight taller than the steeple of nearby First Methodist. In fact it is six feet taller, about the same length as Stanley Booker, there, sitting in the front row, or of Clifford Duncan who I see there in the back row, each good-sized men. Certainly we are not in a race against our brethren at First Methodist to build the highest steeple. Still, we may allow ourselves a brotherly pleasure in being the taller of the two.

"The congregation might find itself alarmed to learn that while its own steeple is taller than the steeple of First Methodist, it is in fact not the tallest point in Shady Valley Town. The tallest point lies at the southern limit of Main Street. There Shady Valley Feed and Grain rises rather grotesquely higher than our own steeple—the length of two good-sized men standing one on top the other.

"The Lord above anyone knows a good carpenter measures twice and cuts once. Though I have measured carefully not twice but several times, it is not for me to cut. My measurements are simply a testament, and I bring this testament in good faith before you today.

"'How to Measure.' Call it the title of today's sermon if you will. It is a human endeavor, the wish to know the length of one's reach and the depth of one's vision. It is a human endeavor to wish to know the dimensions of one's community—the heights of its peaks and the depths of its valleys—and by these dimensions to know its integrity. When we measure the things that we love, we do so with great care and precision. We notice that even a sixteenth, like the head of a small boy, is vital, and in good faith we would never ignore a single sixteenth in our truest measure.

"Friends, as your humble servant, I offer you not what I can build, sow or sell, but only what I can bear witness to. I have but one pair of eyes to witness and but one voice to record. Thankfully, ours is a town of many voices and many points of vision. We see that our population marker out along the Blacktop reads 1,000, yet not 900 souls fill our streets. One soul less this day. A cut has been made. We mourn. We take comfort in the shelter of this well-built house. We take comfort in knowing that the Lord is a sober carpenter. Each tick on His measuring tape is precious.

"And now, may the Lord bless you and keep you, may the Lord lift up His countenance upon you and give you peace. Amen."

Connie

Over time, most of the memories faded and Connie sometimes doubted if they were really his at all or if they were just memories of pictures or memories of other peoples' stories about Dale. Everybody had a story about Dale. He was crazy.

Connie finally got to have Dale's bedroom. All Dale's stuff was still up high in the bedroom closet, his yellow running shoes with the tips going up, his dog tags, his Mexican belt, all his trophies. Connie could reach the picture album up there with all the crazy pictures of Dale: as a kid dressed in a white sheet for Halloween, in a black robe with bare legs and feet outside the high school, as a Marine doing a handstand in his dress blues. In the pictures, Dale had blond hair and blue eyes, like his dad. Connie's hair and eyes were only brown.

One of the pictures showed Dale riding his snowmobile through the yard with no snow. That crazy son of a bitch. It was autumn and the yard was full of fallen leaves but there was no snow. The leaves swirled around Dale as he zoomed hell-bent across the snowless yard on his black snowmobile.

Animal Husbandry

Boil about a handful of hay in three gallons of water; give it to the horses when cold, or, if the cattle and horses are any ways ill, give it to them blood warm. The cattle and horses do not seem to like it at first, but if they are kept very thirsty, they will drink freely of it afterwards.

—*The Citizens and Farmer's Almanac*, 1801

Farmer and Farmer's Radio

Farmer isn't one of those farmers who seems only on the exterior to be simple. Farmer is, though, a farmer, your typical hayseed. Here is his secret: Farmer has lived with women only long enough to know that he cannot live without them. Here is our secret: Farmer needs to forget his stupid secret, he needs his radio. He is only depressed about this one woman anyway, this Sally. Some toe fetish with her. Good riddance to bad rubbish, he should say. We can't talk to Farmer, though, so we can't convince him. We can only watch him muck around in the sloppy. We can only hope his radio keeps him alive, serves as a breath support system: poor quality of breath, but breath nonetheless.

We should butt out of this story. Let Farmer be.

But first here's something we need to remember: Farmer is a dairy farmer. Dairy farmers, like many insects we know, do the same thing every day of their adult lives until they die, or until they sit down to die. Dairy farmers have no hump days, no weekends, and generally not much to holler about.

They do change of course, let's not be naive. They can become alcoholics, liars, church deacons, bookies, bankers, railroad engineers or any number of engrossing and worthwhile occupations. But it takes them a dreadful long time. We must remember that dairy farmers are patient folk who are willing to live poor and meager lives in order that their grandchildren's lives aren't so poor and meager. This selflessness is a religion with dairy farmers. It is also a standard which not all children of dairy farmers can live up to, so many lead guilt-ridden lives. Many also abandon ship; this may be a good thing, for the world's millions can drink only so much milk.

Our point is that dairy farmers change little. In order to measure some reformation in a dairy farmer you have to watch them for something like a lifetime. (You have to watch close too, for if a dairy farmer does change, it's bound to be subtle.) Best just to watch one at chores time, when he's actually doing something. Of course we always hope something implausible will happen, knowing full well that if some change does occur, and we're watching close enough to notice, we'll be privy to something most folks only read about in books. Still, our hope is a potato farmer's hope that his plants will sprout pumpkins. That said, here's Farmer—your typical hayseed—waking up for morning chores.

Farmer can't live alone.

And yet here he is alive at five and facing the prospects of another day of farming, alone. Here he is awake upstairs in his farmhouse. The house radio is on: news. Farmer is covered with a thin sheet from his toes to his moustache. It is amazing, he thinks to himself, I am alone, but still alive. I am tired. Hoo boy. He always feels sorry for himself first in the morning. He tells his durable toenails they need a clipping. They do. He tells his hairy toes to wiggle. They do. I am lonely, he thinks, and my toes have hair. So does my back, my inner ears, the tip of my nose. It must grow when I sleep. No one wants to kiss my hairy toes. It is no wonder I'm alone. Hoo boy.

To make it through the 24 long hours in every day, Farmer needs noise. He doesn't know it, but he does. Farmer socks his feet white. He shivers. He thinks that winter is coming. Farmer hates winter. He hums I'm a little teapot. Lies back down. His life has become a clutter of noises that protect him from unhealthy thoughts, from any thoughts, really, save idle ones. The radio plays all day, all night. Doesn't matter which station. The noise is simply a string that strings through all things. This keeps Farmer listening just enough to bother breathing. It also keeps him from listening to himself and doing something drastic.

Farmer finally gets his ass out of bed. Comes downstairs. Do I feel like blueberry jam this morning?

Silence is the enemy of Farmer because it breeds in his mind a cacophony of wild thoughts about the one woman who has loved him back. Whenever he thinks about this girl, this Sweet Sally, he decides that the better part of his life is over, that another girl will never love him back, that he isn't very smart, that his jaw is too Jersey and his head too Holstein, and even that he's a lousy farmer. Here he is 39. It's no wonder he needs noise then, to keep these shitty thoughts from his mind at five a.m. lest he decide not to get up at all.

Farmer is up and about. He goes to the porch and sees his farmer clothes hanging on hooks. The crotch is gone in these bibs. Do I have to wear these lousy bibs? The coffee pot is dripping. Gurgling. Farmer puts on a flannel, the crotch-less bibs, his shit-covered boots, his shit-covered seed hat. Pfizer Genetics. This is my handle, this is my spout. I am a lousy teapot, he thinks. I am a lousy farmer.

He sits down to breakfast. He places a telephone call to Shipper. Yup, she's alive. Least she should be. Come and haul her off. Hurry, she won't last, he tells Shipper Man. He doesn't want to call Dead Wagon. He slurps his coffee. Next he calls Banker. Tells Banker he lost another cow. Says it's OK, she's breathing. Says he can get six hundred for her. Yes, he knows he paid twelve. Yes, he knows that's three gone already this fall. Says don't worry. Agrees it's a crying-fucking shame. Says don't worry. At least he didn't have to call Dead Wagon. Says sure stop by after golf. Says Old Style sounds good to me. Says so long.

He slurps his coffee. Between drinks, he drags on his Marlboro cigarette. It makes a slight hissing. Coffee and cigarettes, the drone of the radio upstairs, some news: noise. Farmer thinks, I would look like the Marlboro Man if my bibs were better. He decides he will have new bibs next milk check. He decides he will be even better than Marlboro Man. Marlboro Man is a wimp. To hell with Marlboro Man, I am Farmer Man. To afford his new bibs, he will spill water into the bulk tank. Milk Man won't mind. Hell, skim milk is in.

He walks outside. It is late October, and winter is coming. Farmer tries not to think about winter. He snuffles. He thinks he might be getting a cold. The crops are in. The cows are by the barn, mooing a blanket of breath. Some mornings, Farmer wishes he had a goddamn rooster. He remembers one day having a goddamn rooster when this farm was Pa's farm. Hardworking rooster kept the hens' backs bald. Farmer will have a rooster, but no hens.

Some days, Farmer empties both barrels of his shotgun into the air, follows the flight of the wadding. His ears ring, and he heads for chores. Some mornings he wants to sit on the shotgun, pull the trigger, and choke on his guts. This morning he finishes his cigarette, has some more blueberry taste from his moustache, saunters like a cowboy. Time to go to work: he walks the 50-odd paces to work. Farmer has a sense of humor about this. Flicks on the barn radio, breaks the breaker. Flips on the breaker. Comes this noise. Flicks the barn light. Comes this lightness. Comes this routine.

Paul Harvey radio rerun. He walks down the aisle. Walks up to the body of Pretty Holly. The aisle is full of her. She hasn't moved much. Her hip is torn apart. Her leg bones jut. Her blood is frosted with barn lime. He checks; she is breathing. He walks to the end of the aisle, slides the barn door through the sloppy. It squeaks. The sloppy is frozen on top. The cows shoulder in, moo on. They can't wait to get inside to shit on the freshly limed aisle. The fresh piles have breath. Even shit can have breath. Like steaming porridge, Farmer thinks for the umpteenth time. The cows move into their stanchions, head to manger. They step daintily around Pretty Holly. When all but three of his stanchions are full, Farmer knows all of his cows are in. He slides the big sliding door back through the sloppy. He pauses and catches a quick glimpse of the direction east. Everything is frosted to the east.

The cows eat and shit into the gutter. They hunch up and piss straight across the aisle. They aren't careful who's in the aisle. They aren't careful about Pretty Holly. Breath comes from everywhere. The barn begins to warm. Farmer unzips his bibs. He pisses into the gutter onto an Old Style can. His piss looks green. It makes a familiar hollow noise on the empty can.

This is my handle, this is my spout. Wiggle, crouch, zip. And now you've heard—he says along with Paul Harvey—the rest of the story. He clips cows' collars. Their long tongues grope and teeth grind grain. Everything is breathing.

The night before, cows out to east pasture, Farmer made 47 small piles of shell corn and soy protein in the mangers. This is a reason why the cows crowd around. It is just the same food as always, as always food just the same.

The barn becomes filled with the noise of static, and Farmer moves the dial on the radio wired to the barn ceiling. He can't see the numbers because they have been whitewashed over by J.B. Peabody Whitewashing. A dandy job, a really dandy job. The barn is white all right. Still white. Milk white.

He lands on a country station first. A low voice sings. I'm a little bit country, she's a little bit rock and roll. Farmer likes this song but it makes him think about Sally. Rock and Roll Sally. Farmer thinks about how he went to the old wooden bridge over Shady River after Sally dumped him. SALLY SUCKS TOES, bragged the bridge when he left, speaking in silver spray paint. She never had, really; she said she wouldn't kiss those hairy toes, not for nothin'. But now the bridge says it is so, and all those passersby believe it. Everybody believes what they read. But Sally, the toesucker-who-wouldn't, never objected. Farmer fears it popularized her in Bergamot rather than defamed her. He sees her in his mind's eye with a new bounce and lightness that suggest she's proud of her new popularity. It would be nice to be talked about, he thinks. Hoo boy.

That was a year ago. Today Farmer dances down the aisle to the milk house, his boots mixing barn lime with fresh shit. I've got spurs that jingle, jangle, jingle. He thinks he looks good dancing and imagines someone peering in a barn window at him and thinking to herself: that's my kind of man, a working, dancing man. I must have him. Yes, oh yes.

Farmer goes to work in the milk house. He mixes the udder wash. The water is scalding, but his strong hands are used to it. He fills the tit dip. The pump goes on, loud, loud. The milk machines come out. Farmer milks three at a time. Janey, Miss Piggy and Dairy Queen are first. He gently washes their udders. Some of them dribble with anticipation. Tocktock tocktock tocktock, go the vacuum regulators, Farmer's metronome. The milk begins to burst forth into the pipelines. Farmer is proud as his milk bursts forth to the world. Drink milk, he thinks. Drink milk for your teeth and bones.

DQ milks a ton. Miss Piggy takes a swipe at him, mad cow, but Farmer is too quick. Her foot misses his head. Whoa Bossy. Down and on down the line goes Farmer. He maneuvers the step saver around Pretty Holly. Freely flows the milk. Farmer has noise, action, production. His hands move deftly at their business. He soothes his cows and rubs his shoulder on their girths. He tells his cows it's gonna be all right today. Starts to believe it himself.

Halfway down the line is Missuz Shirley, his only red cow. He puts an extra link of the barn cleaner chain on the milk machine to weight it down. She won't milk out and Farmer must massage the last bit of milk out by hand to prevent mastitis. Keep the somatic cell count down, milk check up. A Marlboro dangles from his lips. He massages beautifully. He curls his top lip and sees his full moustache beneath his nose. His scarred hands look strong on Shirley's udders. His shoulders look strong as he squats there in his faded bibs. His sideburns are handsome. His cigarette, manly. Waft, waft, goes the smoke, in a perfect sort of way. What if someone were to walk in the barn and see him looking robust and handsome and rugged there under Missuz Shirley the Red. What if she thought he was just what she needed, someone sturdy and silent and knowledgeable about farming and with a vocabulary including mastitis and somatic cells and, yes, oh yes, artificial insemination. What if...What if all this and Holstein cows piss pure platinum?

He remembers having this thought under Red Shirley last night, the previous morning. The night before, too? Yes, many times. No girl since Sally has walked into this barn. No girl ever will again. Missuz Shirley, who has lain in her piss all night, picks a bad time to swat a fly. Her wet switch slaps across Farmer's face and he tastes her acid piss on his lip. He grunts, flings the milk machine across the aisle, lands a boot on her hock, sinks a fist in her thigh. Gets this wild idea. Reaches to the pipeline, snatches his cow cane and brings it down on her spine. Wham. Again and again, even as she pulls against her collar till her eyes bulge out, he swings. Wham. He suddenly stops. Tocktock, tocktock, tocktock go the vacuum regulators. He hears them over the drone of the radio, which fades in and out. He is sweating, breathing heavily.

The cows have their business ends in the gutters. They moo, dissenting. The shit is flying. Pretty Holly manages to lift her head. You ridiculous idiot, Farmer. He is hot and takes off his flannel. He is ashamed. He is glad there is no one here to see him. He waits for his cows to quiet. They look at him with large, distrustful eyes. Farmer thinks that maybe he's nuts.

Farmer milks on. He is tired of thinking about himself and thinking about women. He is tired of losing control of himself, beating his animals. He is tired of all these cows. He is tired of washing their tits everyday when all they do is shit on them again anyway. He will never make them give enough milk. He will never please Milk Inspector. He is tired of being a lonely lousy nitwit farmer. He doesn't want to be his pa's boy anymore. He is tired of being alone and wishes he had a woman. One with soft hair and pretty fingers. Yes, oh yes, one of those. He can't live without one. But he won't have one. He may as well crawl into his bulk tank and curdle there. Farmer may as well ferment. He is tired of being a dairy man. Tired of being what he does. He is tired of being Farmer.

But he kneels by the shit-filled gutters just the same and breathes the scents of his livelihood. He begins to daydream as he handles the milk machines, fitting the cows' finger-sized nipples into the rubber sockets. Farmer thinks he'd like to milk himself. He imagines milking himself to death. He sharpens his old pocket knife enough to clip the ends of each finger. He does it just the way he clipped the tails from all those blind and mewling pups, born from so many farm bitches that dropped their litters in his hay mow. Except his finger-ends bleed when he cuts them. He inserts each dripping finger into a socket of the milk machine. It takes two machines for his eight fingers. A milk machine dangles from each hand as he stands in the barn, rocking to the metronome. He can see the blood surging through the clear lines of the milk machine and he imagines it is just now hitting the bulk tank, where it mixes with those gallons and gallons of white, where his blood mixes with the milk of the world.

Farmer comes to.

There is no miraculous power surge. Farmer moves under his animals, finishing his milking. But the wax slowly melts from Farmer's ears and he hears his radio. The static disappears. A familiar radio voice, crisp and alive, rises. One of Farmer's favorites. *This is Orion Samuelson with today's livestock report*, goes the radio. Tocktock Tocktock Tocktock goes the last vacuum regulator on the last milk machine on the last cow. And so Farmer rises from his chores. He rises from the same gutters that his pa had risen from, and his pa before that. He rises not alone but along with the pork bellies and winter wheat, along with the spring peas, shell corn and soy futures. Farmer rises even as the milk prices miraculously rise three cents and the pitch of Orion's voice seems to rise a whole octave as he spills this incredible news. And as Farmer rises, he has a vague inkling that this was supposed to happen. He has a vague inkling that God sent Orion Samuelson through his radio to lift him from his haunches. God save you, Farmer catches himself whispering. God save you, Orion Samuelson, for saving my farm.

Farmer has had his epiphany; now it's time to get back to work. He slides the barn door through the sloppy and unclips cows' collars one by one. They back into traffic and shoulder out to east pasture, leaving last piles on the now-green floor. They stumble over Pretty Holly and kick her in the head. Farmer closes the cow yard gate behind them, goes back into the barn to finish chores. He is a little dizzy. He cleans his milk machines, making sure to let the water from the line cleaner run into the bulk tank. He finishes in the milk house, scrapes and limes the barn floor. In the way is Pretty Holly, who is dusted a second time with barn lime. He notices she is about dead, wonders, Where the hell is Shipper?

Farmer flicks on the old barn cleaner, breaks the breaker. Flicks the breaker and the chains begin to grind around on their sprockets. The gutters begin to bubble and move. The shit is heaved forward and augured out to the shit spreader in the cow yard. Farmer waits by the auger head with his pitch fork. He helps along the globs of shit, straw and twine so the auger won't clog. The barn cleaner is grinding away, but Farmer recognizes the voice of The Man in Black on the radio: *I taught the weeping willow how to cry, cry, cry.* Farmer likes the sound of that song, but it makes him sad just the same. It also makes him sad that he has to get through the rest of the day. He decides he will. He will grind through it. He lights a smoke. He gets an image of Sweet Sally at the Best Shot. Rock and Roll Sally. Long brown hair, murderous red fingernails.

Farmer decides to run the shit out. He climbs on his pa's old Farmall and motors out to the field. He has a full load and it slops over the side of the spreader with every bump. Farmer notices that east has melted and the sun has moved up in the sky. There is still a chill in the air. Winter is coming. He squints and starts to think about Pretty Holly. He will have to deal with her. He will have to call Shipper again. He hopes she isn't dead.

Farmer is sick of all this death on his farm. Pretty Holly makes three already this fall. This winter will be worse. He remembers last winter and the thirty-below days that wiped out a dozen calves. He remembers their bodies frozen in their calf huts; the new calves that came would have to bed down on the frozen bodies of the dead. He remembers all the cats and kittens crushed under the cows they had crowded under for warmth. The cows that slipped on ice and ruptured udders, stepped off tits or broke legs. The heifers freezing out in the field. So many bodies frozen to the ground where they dropped. Farmer walked over them until spring. Sometimes their dead bodies fell in advantageous places—one by the spreader he used as a step, one by the gate he used like a gate weight. He had become used to all that dying. Something will die today, he would think most mornings.

Farmer doesn't feel used to it now. He lights a weed and tries to think about how good he looks chugging across the field, bouncing along nonchalantly in the old tractor with the metal seat. He can't seem to get much joy from this image.

He motors back up to the barn and parks the spreader where it belongs under the auger, heads into the barn to call and light a fire under Shipper's ass. He doesn't bother. He finds Pretty Holly has died in the aisle. First thing he thinks about is that six hundred bucks gone. Next he thinks about winter coming again and all the dying that will go on. Next he thinks about how he has kept her alive there suffering these twelve hours just so he could collect on her. You sad ass, Farmer.

Farmer looks down at the body of Pretty Holly and doesn't know what to think. Somehow this cow gone, this tragedy, only makes him feel like he is more unlucky for losing Sally, for being alone. Why does it always have to be about her? He doesn't understand. When cancer ate his pa's throat, he was wondering if that would make Sally love him more. Now he's wondering if she'll walk into the barn and take him back because this cow has died. Farmer thinks he might be nuts. He takes his cap off and rubs his head. He paces the aisle. He shuffles. The radio has gone fuzzy and now sounds like a car race. Every few seconds a loud sound will creep up on the steady low sound and whoosh past it in a buzz of static. Farmer feels like the slow sound that is being lapped again and again.

Then Farmer moves his feet. He moves them to the milk house where he finds his milk machines. He turns on the vacuum pump. It roars loud, loud. He carries a machine down the aisle. He plugs in the small blue vacuum regulator and unravels the hoses. The metronome joins the cacophony of noises. He works fast, freeing Pretty Holly's generous udder from beneath her, washing her. He kneels in her frosted-white blood. Even at the awkward angle, he manages to attach the milk machine to Pretty Holly. And the milk comes forth from her dead udder and surges into the machine and through the bowels of his barn, of his pa's barn, and his pa's before that.

The milk comes fast and fluid and pure. He milks her, dead there on the center aisle of the barn. And he is being lapped again and again by that static sound on the radio. And the vacuum pump roars and the metronome tocks weakly. And amid the din, Farmer is able to think. He is doing something he has never in his life done before nor imagined doing nor heard about being done. He looks there on the dirty barn floor and he doesn't see Pretty Holly any longer. He sees his heart, large and hairy and deformed. He sees his heart dead there. And he sits down beside it to massage forth the last drops of life.

Boar Taint

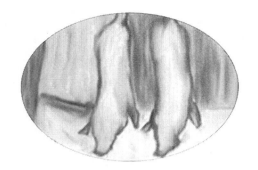

Coasting down the eastern face of the Sierra into Nevada, I saw one final glimpse of California in the side view mirror. So long, bad dream. Slide into the ocean and be lost to its depths. You are hardly a state at all to me now but a woman I still love there. Your stunning granite coastline and verdant interior, your honest to goodness lighthouse smile, your two ripe curves of bottomland that still make me weep, and your ankles, I swear, just thick enough to make you legal—all in the undeserving hands of some other rummy. And here I am about to cut pigs in Odette County, Wisconsin.

I just washed up on the shores of Wisconsin last night, sailed across country alone, and now I stand in an old home farmyard facing my second spring. Wisconsin in June is in full bloom. Can you feature it? There's even an air of lilac, this while the California lilacs are already two months in the hole.

There's Landis Tabor getting off the tractor now. He hops lightly down. Jeans and a flannel, shit-covered high-tops, a halo of golden hair loose below his seed cap. He's not exactly your picture-book clodhopper, but give him a dozen years. Landis walks up and greets Henry and me. Henry—Hen—is my friend along for this errand. Landis doesn't say anything. Just saunters over to stand beside us silent and take the place in. First thing I notice is Landis's farmhouse still fixed with ugly asphalt shingles. Typical farmer what shuns the coop. You ought to know better, fool farmer.

Landis finally invites us in through the mudroom to the kitchen where Marlene, his wife, fixes vittles. She seats us at the kitchen table and serves sunnyside eggs, sizzled bacon, watery coffee and tall glasses of fresh, cold milk. There's no honest vegetarian in the world doesn't love the smell of sizzled bacon, and just when was the last time I drank cold milk dipped from the bulk tank?

How did you know I like my eggs sunny? says Hen.

I get better tips if I cook right, says Marlene.

I keep my nose in my plate, savoring the novelty of bacon, trying not to look at Marlene. She breezes out of the kitchen to the living room where she has the morning news playing on a big console set. From the living room I hear a snippet about the Russian sailors suffocating in their submarine on the ocean bottom. This story of the doomed Russians who had sunk too far to be raised up again has followed me like a rank easterly all the way across the country.

Landis holds his fork like a shovel. I feel bad for noticing. Hen's getting the lowdown from Landis on who ended up with whom. We all come from this same patch of earth; Hen and I were classmates at Shady Valley. Landis was a few years ahead of us and Marlene a few years behind. Hen and I have been flung all over the country, and we now find ourselves reunited after these fifteen years. Landis has been a farmer all the while. He never left Odette County, apparently. Marlene either. I suppose it makes sense that the ones who never left would graft together, never mind the age difference. Here we all are regardless, huddled around the small table in his small farm kitchen drinking milk so fresh it was weighting an udder just this dawn.

Marlene has a cigarette burning in an ashtray on the counter. She doesn't take it with her when she goes to the living room to look at the sad news. There's a red smear on the white filter. Marlene has this gorgeous long black hair I wrapped in my numb hands a few hours earlier. And here she is a farmer's wife, this raven beauty.

We finish eating and Landis says I should borrow some bibs. But he hesitates before handing them over. Are you sure you can get dirty? he says.

I'm diabetic, I say, not mysophobic.

What's mysophobic? Hen says.

Fear a dirt, I say, and rub egg yolk onto my napkin.

You'll never get the smell of hogs out of your clothes anyway, Landis says. But you might as well cover them up.

I'm wearing just shorts and a T-shirt, some white tennis shoes. Inappropriate, to be sure, but who plans to cut hogs hung over on a Saturday morning? I only made the plans some six hours earlier in the small hours of my welcome home party at Hen's. In his toast he said it was good to have me back where I belonged. But he wasn't quite convincing. Everybody knows you can't go home again. I never thought I'd live here again and so far it doesn't seem as if I do. I'm just here doing the tourist gig, laying the farmer's wife, castrating his hogs.

Landis had made the offer last night. I'm getting out of hogs, he said. Stones off the last batch tomorrow. He tipped his beer at me. Didn't you always say you wanted to see inside a hog operation?

As a matter of fact I did. Now more than ever. I told the welcome wagon about a book I had read on corporate farming and the rise of animal cruelty. The author argued that your family farmer respected his livestock because he had to look it in the eyes before killing it. There is no such gaze occurs on these corporate farms where the pigs are crammed nose to tail on metal grates their whole lives—pigs so depressed they let their pen-mates gnaw their tails off without moving. Now most people don't even see skin on their neatly packaged meat, let alone its eyes.

If I was going to eat meat again—and I damn-well planned to now that I was moving back to the farm country—I was determined to recapture the gaze.

No one seemed to be listening to my lecture except Landis. I realized I was proselytizing when the mood called for good-old-days drunk talk. In any case, I certainly didn't plan to arise early for a neutering. Landis said no butchering was happening, but I was sure welcome to come make eyes at his hogs. Across the table, Marlene was already making eyes at me. Eyes Landis may have seen. I was about to beg off when Hen said it sounded fun.

Let's go, Hen said smiling. You're back, you might as well dive right in.

I'm surprised you showed, Landis says now while I pull on his too-small bibs in the mud room. I can't tell if he's condescending or genuinely surprised. You can never tell with these silent farmer types just how much they know. They can endure so much more than the rest of us. He pours the last of the coffee in his barn mug. He was up early, already milked and out spreading manure when we drove up at eight a.m. Of course he was early to bed as well, fool farmer.

I said I'd be here, didn't I? I feel some of that old workman's pride: out late, up early. Anyway, I'm still good for my word, if not much else. Four hours ago I had sex with this farmer's wife folded over the toilet at Hen's. Add home-wrecker to the list of bad things I am. It doesn't matter any longer. There aren't any rules for the lone steer. The trick now is to make each day disappear. The days disappear more quickly with your two hands full of trembling flesh.

This is going to be fun, Hen says. It's no trouble prying my cheerful friend loose of a smile. His fields are sown in straight rows, and he seems so much like a boy to me still. You see the happily married and you don't know whether to envy them or weep for them what's coming. He's been talking with Marlene in the living room, comparing their views of the news, but now he's pulling on borrowed bibs as well.

No fun for the pigs, Landis says. You'll see. Unlike my friend Hen, he's been where they are. We have much in common, I sense, and we could be famous friends if I hadn't done what I did.

In the mud room I pull rubber boots over my shoes. The smell of the mud room reminds me of other mud rooms. Manure and lead-based paint. Hyacinths and biscuits. Everyone I grew up with had a mudroom, whether it was a farm or not. You needed a place to take off your muddy boots in the spring or fall, or to shake off the snow in the winter. No one in California has a mudroom, and this good smell is all lost to them. My colleagues at the agency joked I was coming back to cheese and beer. Little did they know the small linoleum pleasure of a good mud room. Landis's got his chest freezer out here too, just where it belongs. I know if I open it I'll find white packages of butchered meat stacked like cord wood on the frozen vegetables and a tub of Rocky Road from the yellow truck what comes around.

Before we head out Landis hands me a green and yellow seed cap notched too small for my head. Marlene has been quietly cleaning the breakfast dishes, but now a small sob erupts and gives her away. She looks up, wiping her eyes. She's looking right at me, and I look away, feeling myself flush.

What is it, honey? Landis asks. He moves to comfort her. Hen and I haven't manners enough to duck out while Landis consoles his wife.

Oh, it's nothing, she says. But she can't leave it and another small sob erupts. It's just those poor men trapped down there under all that water. They're all going to drown.

Actually they'll suffocate, Hen says, before I can push him out the door.

The low white farrowing house sits across the road. I've always been partial to these farms where the house and outbuildings are separated by a thin strip of road. Someday, I'd like to have a farm like this one. They seem to have a special kind of order and openness, inviting each passerby into the midst of their commerce. The arrangement also offers a suggestion at least of the separation between living and working. Who wants to look out their bedroom window and see the milk-house door yawning?

Landis emerges from the asphalt-shingled farmhouse shaking his head, and we follow him across the road. A cow barn with its silo and corn crib also stand on the grounds, along with two dilapidated machine sheds, but the tallest building is the satellite tower periscoping over the trees. Landis rents this tower to the cell phone company for a small monthly sum. Landis wears his own cell phone in his hip pocket like a snuff tin. He takes us in the farrowing house through the half-cocked gate and gets things ready for the cutting.

Stepping into the farrowing house is like ducking into the hold of a ship. The door header is so low I have to crouch to enter. Inside, I still can't stand up straight and the ammoniac odor is deadly. There are six sows and six litters of piglets. All the farrows scramble round the sows, big mamas laid out so their tits are free. The place has been whitewashed, but not since I was born, and cobwebs cover the windows, the bare bulbs, the circuit breaker. A small transistor radio with a clothes hanger for antennae seems held to the rafters by the cobwebs alone. And there's the trusty Almanac hung on a nail. Baling twine and feed sacks drape every jutting edge, and the corners are stacked in milk-house junk crusted with barn lime. Pale green shoots erupt along the walls, the outside getting in.

Don't get too close to the sows, Landis says. They get a hold of you they won't let up. Leave a nasty tear. He rolls the sleeve of his flannel to show proof: a shiny, grape-colored scar devouring his elbow.

There isn't much room in the center aisle to avoid the sows, but Landis moves easy, getting the tools ready. He stands up just fine in here. On a wooden stool in the center aisle he sets out a silver hypodermic gun which he explains is used to shoot antibiotics into the piglets.

You've probably used one of these before, hey? Landis says.

I don't answer but instead heft the big gun which bears no resemblance to my small disposable hypodermics. There's also the scalpel, some rags and a bottle for suckling calves now red with iodine.

Who wants to catch and who wants to cut? Landis says.

I'll catch, Hen says immediately. The race always goes to the certain.

I guess you're cutting, Landis says, and hands me the scalpel.

The scalpel feels light as a pen. This aluminum scalpel is the exact instrument I held in my first ad room job, where we still did the actual cut and paste. I'm relieved. Though my fingers are mostly numb, I know I can handle this.

I'll cut, I say, but hadn't you better demonstrate? You don't want me cutting anything I shouldn't.

All right, Landis says. I'll cut the first batch, and you hold them.

Neither Hen nor I can tell the difference between the male and female piglets, so Hen has to catch them and hold them up for Landis to sex. While he's after them, they cease their little grunts and begin to shriek. He finally nabs one and carries it by the ribs over to Landis. There is no way to describe a pig shriek except as deathly sincere. The shrieking is immediately the worst of this barbarity. The high pitch bouncing between the close walls deafens me. If you're fatalistic like me you're always on the lookout for triggers, what will it be that finally sets you over. Low roof driving a primitive pig shriek right to your ears will boil the meat in your nut every time.

Aren't there ear plugs or anything? I say to Landis, but I don't think he hears me and in the noise I'm not even sure I've spoken aloud. Where is my voice?

Landis takes the piglet from Hen and holds it up by one rear leg as it screams.

Gilt, he says, and hands the piglet over to me.

I must look dumb because Landis says, Gilt, female. Boar, male.

Boar seems like an awfully rough name for these little fellows. I wonder briefly why there isn't a special name for the little pink males, like there is for the females, the gilts. The gilts get off easy, for the time being. Today, it's the boars that have it coming. I mark this gilt across the back with a thick red grease crayon so Hen won't have to catch her again. He's at work at the hind quarters of the first sow trying to nab the slippery farrows. He's too tentative, and when he lays his hands on them they slip away.

It's a comic scene. Go get 'em Henry, I yell, but no one hears.

The next piglet Landis pronounces a boar, who knows how. He hands me the male piglet by a hind leg and I flip it over and hold its forelegs open while Landis injects it inside the foreleg with the silver gun. Poor bugger can scream. Next I sit on the tiny stool and cradle the piglet in my lap just as you would hold an infant, except I pry its back legs apart while Landis gets set with the scalpel. He feels for the small lump of its testicles with his thumb and forefinger, squeezes them gently, and makes a small incision on the tight skin he holds between his fingers. The piglet is hard to hold, and the cut makes him insane. He writhes in my lap, his toothless mouth gumming for my belt even as he somehow increases the fatalism of his scream.

I guess because of the pressure the small pink testicles erupt like grape meat from the incision site and the piglet screams its final scream. I feel my own testicles hitch in sympathy. Landis pulls the little gonads from what there was of a scrotum, cuts the sinewy connecting matter with a swift slice of the scalpel and drops the bloody nuts into the pit of a tall white bucket.

I was set to take these testicles home and prepare them. Now I'm not certain I will. Landis dabs the cut site with two quick dabs of red from the suck bottle and waves for me to loose him. I mark him with the red grease crayon then loose him in the pen with his mother. He mingles among the quick pink bodies and soon only the bright red stain distinguishes him from his siblings.

Hen's already nabbed another piglet ready to sex. Another boar and we repeat the routine. I watch Landis close for when my turn comes. Though I'm implicated as an accomplice in this act, I know it will be different to be the primary operator. We fall into a rhythm, the three of us working well together. Landis says he appreciates our help. Working alone, this operation would take all day, and at this rate we should be able to finish in a couple of hours. I look at the dozens of squirming bodies and have my doubts, unless most of them are gilts.

In between the screaming Landis gives us unsolicited advice on the basics of farrowing hogs: how the prime time to cut a boar is between two and six weeks; how you can cut a full-grown hog but you wouldn't want to; how the meat from an uncut hog gets a rancid taste what they call boar taint; and how a farrow develops teat fidelity within a matter of hours. You take a dozen squirming piglets for a dozen tits, he says, and they'll each find their way to the same nozzle every time. You can make book on it, Landis says, with a smile that looks to me like pride.

First litter cut. Landis says it's time to trade the knife.

I'll catch, Hen says, laughing, and Landis, the man I cuckolded, hands me the knife.

Knee deep in the second litter, and Hen comes up holding a most tiny piglet.

Looks like a runt, I say.

Sure is a runt, Landis says, handling the piglet. Runt gilt. He passes her back to Hen. Put her in the pen there by the door. Marlene'll bottle feed her for a couple of weeks. She keeps all the runts and odd ones alive, where I'd knock them on the head and be done with it. Hell, price of pork, I'd as soon knock them all on the head as feed them up.

Watching Hen sequester the runt, I figure if he is rejected for his deformity then the converse also holds true. I know an injured animal feels his individualism more intensely than a healthy animal. Out of necessity, he develops a certain aloofness and cunning. This is my theory anyway. At fourteen I was diagnosed with type-1 diabetes. It would be incorrect to say that I was shunned by the litter, but it would not be incorrect to say that the disease made me feel my difference. I hadn't planned to ship out west to college and my eventual antiseptic life as an adman. Had I not been marked I would have ended up sticking around Bergamot to work at some garage or construction outfit or dairy barn—and why not? But diabetes colored me different. It somehow cut me off from the working life and I had to make other plans. That wasn't the only thing diabetes did to me. This clodhopper knows I needle up three times a day, but he doesn't know I can barely feel my fingers. I can't feel my own proud flesh except on a rare morning and I've never had sex natural in my whole life without a pill. I took such a pill last night before cramming into the bathroom with Marlene.

The sows barely move, just sometimes swing their massive heads from the sawdust to get a view. They've been through this routine. They know the slop trough is close by and so bide their time. One of the sows has what looks like long pink thumbs dangling from her neck beneath her chin. I point and Landis says, Waddles. They must be some useless genetic hangover, some tits on a boar.

Hen produces a piglet, Landis pronounces boar, and I'm holding the knife. Landis sits on the bench in front of me and pulls the animal's legs apart. I kneel before Landis and the pig. With my left thumb and forefinger, I touch the animal, feeling the skin of its lower belly, numbly roaming there for its testicles. The skin is smooth, and sure enough, though I don't see them, I feel viscous globes floating beneath the skin. It is an odd sensation. I've never felt testicles other than my own, yet I know the feeling exactly. I pinch them together and Landis says, There, you have them, but I already know I have them.

I hold the point of the scalpel to the skin and Landis holds the animal still. I press. I inject myself daily on the scarred fat of my stomach and I know well the pressure required to break skin. The piglet screams. I've made a red line in the skin as Landis had, but nothing erupts from the line despite my pressure. I increase the pressure but nothing happens. I realize I must have somehow got it wrong. Those weren't testicles I felt. I must have cut a gilt.

From my knees, I begin to tip, but Landis catches me. You're fine, the farmer says, you're just not deep enough. There's another layer under the top layer.

Another layer. I put the scalpel back to the wound but, unaccountably, my hand begins to shake. I don't know if I can cut any deeper. Hen has stopped chasing farrows to see if I can do it. He's smiling. I'm kneeling in the center aisle sweating and I can see Hen smiling some encouraging words, but I can't hear him.

Before I drop the scalpel, and I know for certain I will, Landis's hand closes over mine. I watch this happen more than I feel it. My numb hands. Somehow he's holding all the pig's legs with one hand and holding me with the other. Oh, I had underestimated him. We're not helping him with a chore as much as he's humoring us. What's he doing to us?

Those hands. He could catch, hold, inject and cut much better alone. His hand on mine guides the scalpel. I look up and see Landis's cheek near mine, the curl of blond hair escaping from the seed cap and resting on a pink ear, the hair on the nape of his neck mere down. From this angle, the only thing that betrays his age is the slight bunching of flesh leading to the nub of his ear lobe. I realize how handsome he is. God, how preposterous. Who ever heard of such a blond-haired, blue-eyed pig farmer?

I catch a glimpse of his eye glimpsing mine and then I know, he knows. The gaze. Oh mercy, but I recognize it now. I flush hotly. In this animal gaze, I see proof there is some cosmic farmer god that tends us. He picks us up occasionally from the litter and we scream. He handles us and cuts us, then looses us back to the scrambling litter. We look around at the other pink bodies and feel both shame and sympathy. We call out to the bodies for the ones we know—Hen, oh why, Hen? Hen. Are you cut? Are you cut too?—but hearing no answer, clamber for the great mother nozzle, the sweet tasting one we know as our own and clamp blindly to it.

I watch as my right hand under Landis's puts the blade back to the wound. I see it this way: standing in front of the wash basin as a boy with my father standing behind me, holding the soap, my hands limp, his hands over mine, cleansing both our hands. The pig screams again and the flesh erupts and we've made it through.

When we finally leave the farm, I'm in a drowsy daze, mostly deaf, and with a warm foil packet warming my lap. Marlene secured a nest of pink treasures in foil and sent them with me, along with instructions for preparation. I sit quiet and half-awake in Hen's new model sedan with the empty kid seat strapped in the back. It's a half-hour by country roads to Hen's place, and the featureless Wisconsin horizon plays to me like a lullaby. On Hen's car radio, obituaries roll for the lost Russian sailors. I crack my window to breathe, but the air does not seem fresh. Landis is right about that pig smell. It clings to us like our own odor.

Hunting & Trapping

First day of winter. Feels like the hundredth. Snow came early, and now the roads are covered with semi-frozen slush, the sun is hardly to be seen, and a keen little north wind cuts down out of a sky the color of a prison wall.

—*The Old Farmer's Almanac*, 2011

Heartshot

The buzz goes way back beyond. It began with a rich girl, a Piper. A company picnic at The Groves, one of those exclusive hunter's clubs. Indian summer. And as rich daughter's new boy, I'm invited along. Wear those shit-kickers, her father says. He gets a kick out of me, I suppose. Her father has a crew that barbeques maybe a hundred pounds of prime steer. And you should have seen the Benz-driving socialites, all dressed in khaki and suede-patched elbows, proclaiming their long lineage as hunters, tearing at the rare meat. There are guests, but the woods are large. We have the whole privileged acreage to wander, Piper and I. We row on one of many quaint ponds, and I ogle the massive, corn-fed, bucket-mouth bass. I row backwards to the middle and we drift. She, sweaty in the open back of her black dress, leans against my thighs. I finger her matching black choker. Panicked pheasants shimmy from the brush and whinny overhead through the occasional blasting. Along the far edge of our pond, a wadding drops, creates a stir. After rowing, we return to the affluent flock.

First dinner—a trough of meat—then sport. The guns appear from the polished backs of luxury sedans parked conspicuously on gravel and in puddles. These are guns like I have never seen: Brownings and Remingtons with double-barrels over-under and side-by-side. The stocks have a wooden luster and the barrels a bluish hue that holds a certain depth. This boy's shot before, her father says, clapping my back. He can use one of my guns. He unwraps his best gun, a Winchester Grand American, worth, certainly, more than my car. Ever look down the barrel of a Winchester? he says with a wink, handing it over. It is a heavy gun. A side-by-side. I point it up and aim down the barrels. It is mesmerizingly perfect. I swing it around and follow a crow.

There is a level of discomfort. It is the same feeling I had when I first sat in a leather seat in her father's car. Piper and I drove it to get dinner wine—another first, wine with dinner. And Piper made me pull over in a cul-de-sac and climbed on top of me, dress up, before I could stop her, as if I would have. I gripped the wheel and stroked the leather dash and pushed all the gilded buttons until it was over. At the time it felt like something new and valuable, the whole moment galvanized by new car smell.

The crow escapes, and a flatbed truck arrives. Perhaps a dozen of us hunters climb on like school chums. I reach down from the truck to hike up Piper, gunless, wearing a frown. Her backless dress is an angry sleeve. That impeccable sense of equity has been damaged again. She wants a gun.

We follow a tractor path to a sorghum field, each of us standing splay legged to absorb the shock, guns down. We are heavy from the meat. The men are a gaggle of clichés: lawyers, executives, their accountants, all dressed in over-priced hunter vests with the shell and game pouches. Their guns swing natural as brief cases. The men talk about game management, about the taste of fresh game, about harvesting game. I keep my mouth shut. I've never met a hunter yet who admits he likes to make things bleed. It's always about resource management, harvesting a resource. As if they're doing the world a favor by blasting it all to shit. Rich hunters even more so. They act like the world is an old Buick that would throw a rod if it weren't for their driving. The rest of us poor bastards ape them, unaware the joke's on us.

The men pass out long cigars. I decline. Piper's father is their book keeper. Says this to be demure. Says he's a book keeper. Like he doesn't own the fucking joint. The flatbed jostles on. At the sorghum food plot we get off, pair off in fours. A few of the men bleat, Pheasants forever! It's their Semper fi.

Piper slides on a pair of bibs and shit-kickers the guide has extra. She's a farm girl now but for the sequined choker. She skirts the sorghum with me and her father and a man named Mas Vino. That's what his Benz license plate says, Mas Vino. Piper has the ease of her class to call him this. He is a fat pizan. Our guide is a red-haired little man who seems to know his job. He compliments the rich men on their guns, helps Piper into her bibs. Her father and Mas Vino load their guns. Mas Vino has a 12 gauge semi-auto, and her father has a gold-plated Remington over-under. The plan is we'll warm up with sporting clays and then wade the sorghum for ring necks. The ring necks are thick as ticks in the sorghum, the red-haired guide assures, and their distant cackling affirms it.

I have a problem with my gun I am embarrassed to mention. My old J.C. Higgins pump is nothing like this. I've seen guns like this in magazines. I know I can shoot one, but there is that problem of the barrels. There are two barrels, one trigger. Which chamber engages first? Mas Vino and her father each have their turns with the clays. They each nail one of two offerings from Red. Then it's my turn and I have to ask. I don't want a trial by fire.

I don't know which barrel fires first, I say. Old Mas Vino about shits a canoli. Your hayseed can't crack a gun? he says to Piper's father. Mas Vino is this big shit hunter, and I've been to his villa to see all the stuffed animals. There must be more than a hundred species, representing every continent. He's even got this wooly musk ox that grazes in the guest room: a couch with legs. Must have taken a sharp shooter to bring that one down, boy. I want to ask Mas Vino Pizano if he rode the fat, bearded cow before he plugged her.

Her father is embarrassed for me and explains. The first click engages the left barrel. You always shoot the modified choke first. Full choke second. Piper too looks at me strangely, as if I had just asked her how to skin a catfish.

So I have my turn, now that I've got it straight, and nail both the little fucking pigeons, new gun or not. Right barrel, left barrel. Click. Click. Boom. Boom. Clockwork. The careening pigeons split in the sky with the sharp report from the gun. The sound is deafening, and I think it's the sound maybe that breaks the clays. My ears buzz, the start of this. I see no one else is wearing ear plugs, so I don't ask. We fire off maybe twenty rounds, from different angles. I go deaf. Red even sends up some tiny clays, which he calls doves, and I manage to nail those too. I've shot real doves, yanked their sparrow breasts out, and it all comes back to me.

With these clays, my percentage is better than Mas Vino's. Her father, for all his clout, might as well be holding a nine iron. It's the goddamn choke on this new gun, he says. I wouldn't be too afraid of him if I were a ring neck cock, a wild one.

But the birds we go out after aren't wild ones at all. They're raised in pens like chickens, and you have practically to step on them to get them to flush. Then it's point and shoot, an arcade game with real blood and feathers. This is nothing at all like hunting. And I am no hunter, though certainly I have hunted. I witnessed a massacre early, and that soured me to the whole business. But when you live out there where I do, you have to be able to manage certain tasks without blushing: castrate a bull calf, breed a heifer, tie your dog to a tree and plug her square between the eyes if she's got a taste for blood. Those kinds of things. So I learned early how to handle a gun. And my one blessing is I've always had a sure eye, no matter what I'm aiming for. This trait I share with Piper.

We don't have a dog, what with the busy day at the club, and Piper's father tells Piper to go out after the birds we kill. He's just blasted his first one, after four easy misses. By making her fetch our game, he's trying to teach her humility. Like making her work at the club restaurant, summers and weekends home from college. She's a waitress there and all his cronies are her customers. They get drunk, slap her ass and tell her she's a chip off the old gold brick. They scatter sawbucks for tips like they were singles. In all her humility, she brings home three hundred a night—that's more than my haul for forty hours at Shady Valley Feed and Grain.

And now, lesson two, he's sending her out bird dogging. I think, too, that I am part of her humility instruction, some sporting clay to warm up on before the genuine cock arrives on the scene. But I also fear that she's going to get nailed out there in the chest-high sorghum, her smear of lipstick as bright as any pheasant head.

A good bird dog has a delicate mouth, he says to her as she drags his mangled pheasant back up to our group. A good bird dog won't crush the prey in its jaws. I have to laugh at this because there isn't much meat left under the feathers. He shot the bird at point blank with eight-shot, and it's riddled with steel, held together with sinew.

Aim for the head, hey Douglas, says Mas Vino to her father, like her father doesn't know this. He was flying away, her father says. I didn't have the angle. Flying away is the easiest angle, of course, but you have to wait until it's a good distance, so you don't shoot the ass out of it like he's gone and done. Next is Mas Vino's turn and he shoots his bird, cleanly, a few pellets to the eyes. Piper goes and gets the bird and Mas Vino holds it up by its scaly legs to admire. Touché, Vino says, dancing with the bird. Piper beams too, like she's waiting for a bone. Good dog, I whisper, patting her rump. Her eyes cut.

Except for the deep crimson rolling from its beak, the bird looks like it did when it was alive. That's why people hunt birds, of course, because you can't see life in their eyes. It doesn't seem like you've done anything to the bird when you've killed it, like fishing. Cleaning a bird is worse though, and it always shocks you, the sickly warmth of their innards when your hand slips inside.

Next is my turn, and I take the lead in our foursome. It is like golf, this way, each of us taking our turns like gentlemen, the next bird always sure to be there. Actually, I get two to flush, and I shoot the eyes out of the first immediately. I've got a good feel for this gun now, and it feels like the only gun I've ever used, like it's my gun. I wait on the next bird, eye along the barrels, letting him angle off out of the sun. Then I shoot, and the bird takes a sharp angle toward the ground like a hell-bent kite. I get claps on the back for my shooting. I've killed the two proverbial birds. Piper legs off through the sorghum. My ears ring, and I begin to loathe this massacre, but I'm too cowardly not to shoot.

Red has a mesh bag he loads the birds in. After we're through, he says, he'll take them back to the kitchen and have them dressed and packaged in tight freezer sleeves. How cute, I think. We won't even have to get their gamey smell or warm blood on our fingers. Red tells us now that we're only just beginning, that in fifty yards we'll come to the end of the sorghum and up to a picked bean field. The runners will be stacked in those last rows of sorghum, he says. They'll be easy to pick off over the clean field. The runners are those birds that don't fly, the ones that keep just ahead of us in the thick reddish grass. The ones that have managed some bit of native sense, even after caged chicken lives.

We each take another turn before we come up to the edge of the field, haul in two more birds, and Piper is fighting the leash. She's done a good job, she says, and now she wants her turn to fire. She makes this plea to her father, but he won't hear it. This is too much gun for you Pipe, he says. We need to get you started on a four-ten, or at most a twenty gauge. These twelves will knock you on your can. Stand back just this one time, and I'll make it up to you later. He winks at her like he's won. She knows he'll make it up, that she'll win too. This is their little game. The stakes are high, but they both come out smelling rosy no matter the outcome. There are no losers here. So Piper backs off, but she's fuming.

We come within ten yards of the end of the food plot and Red tells us to spread out, that we'll sweep up to the edge in a line, and when the birds flush, it will be a free-for-all. Piper tugs at my sleeve. I can feel her excitement. She says something to me, but I can't hear her for the ringing in my ears. I am beginning to sicken.

I can sense the massacre this will be, like one I've seen before, when I was a boy, when I first got my J.C. Higgins that my grandpa ordered direct from the Penny's catalog. My friends had gotten first guns too and had come over to my house to try them out.

I lived on Shady River then. There were no neighbors near, but a quarter mile upriver was another place. Those people had ducks, but they moved out and left the ducks. Now the gray and white birds would float down river and bivouac in our yard. Ducks like to shit on land, who knows why, and my old man gave us permission to clean up the mess. We had a new dog, a female setter mix named Riley who was supposed to be a bird dog, but young Riley must have been a closet duck lover because she never would hound those birds.

So my friends and I took the duck plugs out of our guns—the first trick we learned when we got them—and headed downriver to hunt. Loaded for bear, we said, five shells each plus one in the chamber. We found the ducks, all dozen or so, back in the woods, on the far riverbank. We made our plan. We'd each shoot one—culling the herd—and one of us would wade out and get the three dead. There would be more to shoot next time. We'd manage the flock this way.

The river was only fifty yards across, and the ducks were practically tame. They quacked when we ambushed them. Lane and Nathan started blasting, but I had my safety on and fumbled at first. In the second or two I lost, my two friends had gone berserk. I didn't even fire. The ducks, pets they were, huddled so close together along the far bank that you couldn't tell where one duck stopped and the next began. Lane and Nathan kept firing into the crowd, which was growing tighter. The ducks were screaming awfully, and my ears were ringing from the blasts, but before too long Lane and Nathan were firing on empty chambers, and there I stood, dumb as a stump. The crowd of ducks was dispersing, some floating quietly downstream, heads under, others waving at us with their giant wings waving for help.

Garbage detail. That was what Nathan called my job then. I waded into the icy water, and for the first time, used my gun on living things. There were five wounded ducks that needed finishing. I did it from close range, and the impact of the shot on their buoyant bodies sent them under water and then up again, like bobber fishing.

My ears rang as I dragged the dead birds up to shore and heaved them at the feet of my friends. There was one duck I hadn't manage to finish. I could feel her heart beat when I picked her out of the water. But then the heart beats ceased. That does something to you, when you feel the heartbeat go like that.

Those ducks made quite a stack—there were eight dead in all. We didn't know what to do with the bodies, so I went back up to the house and got a spade. We buried them under the black forest dirt. I can still see their white bodies and chipped bills, like decoys. I can feel the weight of each of those birds, necks stretching, as I dragged them out of the water. Dead, they looked embarrassed. Lane and Nathan were easy about the whole matter and joked about duck soup, duck ass and duck butter. That seemed to be the end of it.

Didn't take too long, though, for young Riley to find the cache, and pretty soon, we had duck ass strewn everywhere. Worse, Riley got a taste for fowl, and by-and-by it was the chickens from down the road. She certainly didn't have a bird dog's soft mouth. Riley moved up to livestock next, and she'd always have a leg of calf or pygmy goat she'd be gnawing on. My old man said it was my mess to clean up, so that's when I took Riley down to the river and chained her to a tree like you do. She knew what was coming and laid her ears back waiting for it. Then it was her hole I was digging. The whole business made me sick to my stomach, but I was glad to have it over with. That's how my hunting days waned just as they were first waxing.

And now, instead of the river, I'm wading this wine-stained sorghum. And I can feel what is about to happen. In real hunting you never know what's going to fly up, and it scares you sometimes, after hours of nothing, when suddenly there's a flush of life. If you've ever flushed wild turkeys while pheasant hunting you know what I mean, how they crash through the forest without much care for what they might fly into. How it stops your heart sometimes, the suddenness and noise of their flight. There is no underestimating the impression a turkey makes when you're expecting pheasant.

There will be no surprises now. We're within five yards of the edge of the sorghum, and I can feel the life pulsing there, sense the coming explosion. I look out of the corner of my eye and see Red has his arm up. When he drops his arm we'll take a step forward and some of the birds will flush.

I make up my mind then to let Piper have her way. It's a decision I've made just now. I want her to be part of this losing, to know how it feels to do something despicable. To be despicable and to feel shame for it. I want her to learn her lesson from me. Not from her father, who's too far gone to learn anything. She's just a little girl yet, Piper. She's never been away from home, and I'm the only mistake she's ever made.

I know that when she gets her own real troubles, that will be the end of me. She will be weaned from me. Despite everything, though, I've fallen in love with her, hardwired bird: Piper, sand piper, snipe. Yet I'm brutal to her for what she will do to me some day. I'm brutal to her because her father is brutal to me. Because her people have always been brutal to my people. I want her to get some currency from me now. The only thing I have left to give her is this lesson. I can scar her, now.

Her father is beyond both Red and Mas Vino. He's looking out over the clean bean field anticipating. I imagine him keeping book, adding up the final tally even now. I motion Red to wait, then I reach for Piper and pull her close. She whispers something, but I can't hear her for the buzzing in my ears. You'll shoot, I say, and she smiles that smile of hers. I'll guide you. I take her hands and help her hold the gun. I stand behind her and help her train her eyes along the barrel. Don't worry, I tell her. I'll hold on. And I do hold on. I'm behind her as a shock absorber. I hold her tight. She is frail, and I can feel her heart pounding.

Then we step, and wings flap. There is something mechanical in the flush of wings, and for a moment I can hear the rusty squeaking. Then the blasting starts and I help Piper get two shots away. We have managed to hit a bird, I think, unless someone else got that one. I look over at Red and see he's got his gun upside down on his head. He fires, then aims the gun from between his legs and fires again. Next he goes behind his back. The birds keep dropping. He's a fucking circus clown. I could shoot him then. I take the gun from Piper and crack it, slide in two more shells. I'm furious. I hand Piper the gun again and cradle her, shaking, but this time she pushes me away. She wants to do it herself.

I step back. All right. She'll learn her lesson the hard way. Piper steps forward, a ringneck beats it, and she unloads. The gun is too much for her though, and her first shot pushes her backward while the gun points straight up. When your hearing goes, your other senses must go with it, for I'm slow to react. She's still got her finger on the trigger, with the beautiful blue barrels pointed up, when the gun discharges again.

Piper crumbles to the ground like a heart-shot doe. She's not moving. My ears are ringing and the pitch keeps changing, some emergency broadcast. I unfreeze, finally, and go to her.

Piper's face looks angry when I turn her over; it's still locked in that fierce aim. Piper, wake, I say, gently shaking her. I see immediately why she's out cold. There, at the bridge of her nose, between her eyes, is a crescent-shaped cut that's just beginning to well. Looks like a carefully placed killing shot. That, definitely, will leave a scar. The recoil of the gun found a target. I can't suppress this thought: leave it to a dipshit rich chick to get shot by the back of a gun.

Her cut begins to drip now, onto the tiny bruised grapes that are the sorghum seeds. I smear some on my fingers and lick. I am dizzy. I lift Piper's head and cradle it. I loosen her tight choker so she can breathe. She looks like a little farmer doll with her striped bibs. She's got bruised plum cheeks, a delicate mouth, and I can see that some of her crimson lipstick is stuck to the white kernels of her teeth. Next to her is the gun. The barrels shine muted blue, and I wonder how her father left me in charge of something so valuable.

I know her father and Mas Vino will come running soon. Push me over like the clodhopper I am. In fact, I yell for them, because I know I deserve it, but my voice seems tinny, far away. They haven't yet noticed the man down, and the blasting continues. I hold Piper close to me, rare bird. She is soft and pliable. I begin to hope then, a pathetic hope. I begin to hope she doesn't stir just yet. Piper, sleep, I pray. I put her necklace back on, a finishing touch.

I look over her and out beyond the sorghum to the picked bean field, so very clean but for the scattered carcasses. The sky is purpling. Wind carries the scent of something dead. There is a deep and resonant hum that emanates from the lifeless ground. I recognize this finally as the sound shame makes, and it's flying this way.

Every Trapper Knows

You wade into the gray December river, chill pressure pushing against your waders. You're crossing at a shallow spot where Shady River is waist deep, the pressure feeling good against your legs and groin. This is your river, running north, not wide, water clear. Put your face close to the water, you see more than just your face. You see algae-grown rocks at bottom of the river. You wade slowly, checking your balance against the current, using your heavy bodark trapping stick as bottom feeler for boulders and snags. Your rubber waders glide over the slick bottom. Yes, this is your style, slow and stealthy toward the deep middle. All drama arrives in good time. No need to rush and slip and fill your waders with freezing river water.

The water deepens in the middle and shallows as you near the far bank. The pressure lessens. Safely across to the far bank, you look back over the river. Your house, just visible in the morning grayness, sets low and brown through the trees, a long way back from the bank. Smoke issues from the chimney and there's a light in the kitchen.

You wade northward, downriver, against the far, high bank. Your trap line stretches downriver almost a mile from here. You have traps set all along the river bank, under water or just up the bank, a whole line of them, beginning here. You're a trapper, yes, but a fledgling yet, this just your third season trapping. You don't make a living trapping, god no, you've got a job in Shady Valley at the Jake's Lumber Mill for a living. But even at Jake's they tease you, call you Trapper.

Your first trap is a muskrat trap set along the mud bank just under water. This first set is empty. The square steel trap sits over the hole untouched. It always hurts to see a trap empty, especially the first trap. This is a small Conibear over a hole to a muskrat den, the easiest of all sets. You know the hole is active because the river bottom is swept clean from the muskrat traffic. Muskrats are careless swimmers, easiest to trap. You don't bother to camouflage the trap over the hole, nor do you stake it. Muskrats die easily in a Conibear trap.

Now, you wave your trapping stick through the set Conibear and touch the antennae trigger. The trap springs shut on the stick. When an animal swims through the square, brushing the trigger, the trap springs shut and breaks its back or neck. But you have already taken three rats from this hole. You won't take more than four rats from one hole—you have a survivorship ethic—and three is plenty.

You put the sprung trap into your burlap sack, tied over your shoulder with baling twine, and continue on downriver, checking for holes in the bank with your trapping stick.

The current wants you downriver and you want downriver with the current. Your mind springs ahead to the later river, past the bend by the big hemlock, to the willow grove where the beavers eat their midnight lunch. It's the beaver you're after, the big one lurking there. This first upriver part is important, but your mind wants downriver where the current goes. You have to work hard to stake it here, to this important preparatory work.

The next trap holds a dead muskrat. That's better. That quells the downriver current. The brown back and tail of the muskrat float on the water, its head weighted down by the steel trap. It is an easy kill, set much like the first. With your heavy rubber gloves, you reach down into the water, lift the animal and pry it from the trap. You remove a glove and feel the prime pelt, fur thick and intact, guard hairs long and black. You place the animal in your sack, then kneel and reset the trap—it is your first kill from this hole. You can set a muskrat Conibear with your bare hands. It feels good to squeeze the spring with your fingers squeezing against the steel pressure.

The next three sets in the line all hold a prize. There's even a muskrat in the foot trap at the base of a run. The drown set has worked perfectly and you lift the waterlogged muskrat from the middle of the stream and place it in your sack. You reset the foot trap. The foot trap is a good set, more difficult than the Conibears over the muskrat holes. It feels good to take a muskrat in this set, like you're getting better at this, preparing for downriver.

The morning is lightening. The river is opening up. All around you there are signs. Signs, you think, that only a trapper sees. You spot game trails and nipped twigs. You notice a beaver track, like a child's except for the sharp claws that carve the mud. Moving along the high bank downriver, your sack heavy, you imagine yourself as an old trapper—spent-charcoal beard and calloused hands like a steel trap—working alone in some mountains. Trappers work alone. There is no one to blame if you misplace a set or if you're careless about scent. You don't divide reward either.

The river curves in front of you by the big hemlock, finally, and you know you're near the end of your line. It hurts a little, for it to be so early, yet so close to the end. The thin layer of mist over the water is disappearing in the warming air, and soon the mystery will be gone altogether, but not just yet. Here are three beaver sets in a row. You'll take unchecked beaver traps first thing in the morning over anything. Muskrats, sure, but beavers, yes. Somewhere just ahead is the big one you've been looking for.

The first set is empty, the big foot trap nestled in the brown leaves unsprung. You placed it on dry land amidst the willow glade. The beavers are at work here, eating the succulent bark and new shoots of the willows. This is a good place, and you had a good set. You buried a foot trap under a thin layer of loam and leaves beneath a fresh-gnawed willow. This trap should have held a beaver. But scent is a delicate thing on land, and you haven't mastered it—how to get your hands on things and then cover up the scent of your hands. Still, you spring the trap and reset it. The action of the trigger must stay fast, scent or no. If dampness forms on the trigger, freezes on the trigger, even a heavy animal might walk right over it. To reset the trap and place it perfectly takes delicate time. If you conceal the trap too much, it won't kill. If the trap isn't concealed enough, it won't kill.

You re-cover the trap, the wire. You cover your tracks with the bitter scent from muskrat gland, strong enough, you hope, to overpower your own scent.

A new, big tree lies down in the willow glade, just lying there wasted. Each year the beavers eat down the new saplings, and each year the willows grow back. Some years the willow glade grows out to the north; other years it seems to retract to its core. At its core, the big adult willow lies fallen, newly killed. Beavers are excellent engineers, sure, but they're audacious, every trapper knows. Sometimes, a beaver, a really big one, like this one, will fell a big tree just to sharpen his teeth.

Back on the bank, you find the next trap, a drown set, sprung. Only four beavers so far this year, half as many as last, and these small, none over fifty. The hundred-pounder is still out there, sharpening his teeth on big trees. You enter the water again, excited again, feeling the pressure again, like the first time. You look at the mud place on the bank where the trap had been. Now the trap is gone. It's out in the deep water at the end of the wire. You wade out.

This is the good not-knowing, not to be rushed. You had placed a large Conibear killing trap at the bottom of a well-used run, covering it with a light pine bough and weaving on the trigger sprigs of savory willow. So far this season, two muskrats stumbled into the trap. The powerful trap had almost snapped them. A beaver trap can snap a man's arm, but however powerful the trap, it might only stun a beaver, a really big one. You know all about such power, having seen it escape you, so you had set this kill trap to drown as well. You wired the trap to a boulder rooted in the riverbed.

You wade to the rock, only a foot below the surface, and feel under water for the wire with your boot. The water is hip-deep, deep enough. You find the wire and give a short tug. It's heavy. The animal at the end is heavy. This is the one, surely. You savor the moment, imagine pulling the gigantic beaver upstream. Home, you will shoulder the monster, no matter how heavy. Judge at the fur barn will finally believe your story. So far, you're all story. The big beaver will secure your reputation. You pull the heavy load in, feeling the heavy pressure at the end. It's heavy all the way in.

First glimpse and the fur is gray. Another tug on the wire and you recognize the fur, coon fur. It's a big coon, probably forty pounds. But only a coon. No one wears coon skin anymore. Now, the biggest coon in the woods won't buy the trap to catch it.

Using your steel trapper's tongs, you spread the jaws of the big Conibear. The coon is caught square. You pull the coon out. Then, still holding the coon, you reset the trap. You set the powerful spring on each side of the trap and reset the trigger. You place the safety catch on the trigger until you wade back in and set the trap at the base of the run. Then, carefully, you remove the safety catch. The trap sits still.

It's seven a.m. and now is the time to move quickly. The mill opens at eight and you have much work to do. You find the remaining beaver set empty and wade on to the end to check the final two muskrat traps. It had been a good day: four rats and a coon.

At the first of the last two muskrat traps, surprise. You find half a muskrat. The head and forefeet are gone. Weasels have robbed your traps before. The carcass of the muskrat is half eaten. The whole head is missing. You fling the gory carcass out into the current.

At the next trap, culprit. But no weasel, this is a prime buck mink. You suspect what has happened. The predator roams from den to den, hunting muskrats. He filled his belly at the previous hole, easy meal, but no thrill. The mink moved onto the next hole, fattened, arrogant, looking for thrill. He swam right into a lousy muskrat set that hadn't any right to kill a mink. Lucky for you. You hold the mink up, stroke its fur. It has the sleek, long body of a predator, more than two feet long. On its chest is a white blaze that distinguishes it from a weasel. This is your first mink of the season and only the second of your life. Put in your time on the river, every trapper knows, and you'll get lucky before you'll get better. You'll take a lucky mink, and Judge at the fur barn can go fuck himself.

Trudging upriver, you're loaded down by bounty. You drag the coon by a piece of baling twine behind you, and the big dead coon makes a wake in the current. Your satchel overflows. All the extra weight, and the moving upriver, makes for slow going.

Back in the yard, you hang the coon, mink and muskrats by their feet in the old pump shed. You linger here in the pump shed, counting the hanging carcasses. This is part of the pleasure of trapping, being done trapping. Fourteen muskrats, two beaver, four coons, a mink. Two weeks' work. You lock the door to the pump shed.

A big buck mink will fix your luck, or make you think it will, but weather trumps luck every time. It storms the next two days and the temperature dips to ten below. A layer of ice coats the river, the trees. The sun comes out but the mercury stays put. You don't check traps for four days. They're frozen empty anyway. You spend the time on the animals you've already caught, readying the pelts for sale. Someday you might buy the equipment to stretch and tan the hides, but you're not yet invested. You can't sell a pelt frozen wet, so you must thaw and dry the animals first, rising a shine in the pelts. This is the finish work. One by one, you bring them into the house, comb the lice out of their thick fur, and lay them on newspapers in front of the fire to dry. You spend extra time with each animal, feeling its delicate hands, running your fingers over its yellowed teeth. When the fur dries to a shine, overnight, the animals look alive and healthy. You carry the nice-looking carcasses back out to the pump shed and hang them again in the dark shed to freeze.

On a Saturday you make the dreaded trip to the fur barn, hauling a pickup full of furs. The fur barn's just beyond the Odette County line, twenty miles away by frozen gravel roads, and you make three or four trips a season, waiting for the pelts to build up so you can bring in a worthy load.

Inside, the wooden fur barn is frigid. The fur buyer stands on a big pallet behind a high counter laden with fur. You've never seen him before. The fur buyer changes every time so you never know him. Trappers call all the fur buyers Judge. A round man with red whiskers and yellow teeth, this Judge wears many layers of sweatshirts and thin flannels, but his hands are bare, with long knife-like nails. You lift your kill onto the counter. In a moment, Judge will render your kill unworthy and destroy your self-esteem. You know what's coming, but what to do? You're the one wants to be a trapper, and these are the rules. Every trapper faces the Judge. Standing on the pallet, Judge looks bigger than he is. He handles the animals, turning them over in his hands, readying his verdict. A certain duration adds weight to his verdict. Here it is:

The muskrats got mousy fur, on account of these is babies yet, and the winter's too warm to coat a muskrat right. These beavers is nice ones kid, but they ain't quite big enough for the full market. Shady River don't grow no big ones. This mink here is prime buck mink, but see these marks? This mink's been trapped before and chewed his way out. What else we got? Coons? Shit, kid, coons is practically worthless.

What do you say? You say, I think they're worth more. Same as every time. Give me a break, hey Judge. But he don't. You get the feeling he's lying about the fur quality, trying to fuck you, but when it comes from the Judge, you get nervous and full of doubt, and you believe him you're just a kid trapper yet.

You try a new tactic, the threat. If that's all you'll give, hey Judge, I'll take the fur elsewhere.

Then take the furs, Judge spits. You think I need these mousy furs? I got more furs than I can sell. Look at all this fur. He spreads his arms, and sure enough, the fur barn is stocked with fur.

Judge counts out three dollars for each of the muskrats, two for the coons, and fifteen apiece for the beavers. These are all-time lows. The mink brings the highest price, forty dollars. Total comes to one-twenty. Not even what you spent on traps.

I'll feed 'em to the worms before I'm back, you say, and Judge grunts a heavy grunt to say, You feed the worms, kid.

Driving home, you follow the smooth tracks between snow. The gravel road is white but the two tracks. Slouched on the pickup's bench, wrist hung limp over the big wheel, it hits you. You're perfecting a worthless trade. This is the wrong place, wrong time, but here you are anyway, sad-ass Trapper. Sure, everything is swell out on the river. On the river everything else disappears. But there's more to it than the river. You come wading out of the river with a worthless sack of fur. You didn't pick the river. It's the river you were given, grown up here, the only river in this country. All the other trappers skinned out to some other country, Shady River too close by to be any good. So you had it to yourself, big enough river.

But the Shady isn't big enough anymore. There's only so much gold in one small river, every trapper knows.

One thing you've got square. Everything kills something, and if it's going to happen, you'd just as soon see it up close. Judge and everyone else can stand behind the tall counter. Put you in the river any day. But there is the right and wrong of a two-dollar killing. You were never in the river for the money, but there's a difference about throwing money away. The low price shames the animal and the trapper. Only the fat-ass fur buyer makes good. And high class country club women get theirs for cheap.

You park the truck, head inside. No, your furs don't keep none warm in this neck of river, Trapper.

Next day is better. It's always worst just after a sale, but sleeping it off, the river is always there. You take a look at the mercury, but the mercury's still low. You walk out to the pump shed to look at the traps, wondering if you'll extend the line. The sprung traps hang on heavy nails in the shed. It's never been this bad. As you look at your traps, you don't know if you'll take them down again. Hanging from nails, the rows of traps and chains look like torture devices. You decide this is the last of it. This will be it for the season. You'll pull the rest of the traps and let them hang in the pump shed until next season when you can decide whether to take them down.

The river at dusk is frozen and a light snow obscures the ice. You're used to being out here in the pre-dawn. Dusk is not the same. You step onto the frozen river and the ice complains at your weight. You slide out to the middle, pounding the ice with your heavy trapping stick to check the thickness. The ice creaks and groans all the way down the river. The ice is plenty thick, but in the current the ice will be thin. If you break through the ice in the current, you're through. Walking along the far bank, close to the wind, you stop at every set to pull the small Conibears. This will be the end of it. One after the other, you find the empty traps frozen in the ice, their antennae triggers frozen and useless. You chop the frozen traps from the ice with your trapping stick.

Between sets you walk down the middle of the river, checking the ice in places with the stick. On the ice you get downriver quickly. You round the bend by the big hemlock for the last of the traps. Up on the bank, the beaver trap in the willows glade sits covered with snow and frozen to the ground. You break it free, cut the wire lead and stuff the empty trap in your sack. The sack is getting heavy, all the empty traps.

Few tracks mar the clean snow at the willow glade, fewer still out on the river. The storm and cold snap has sent all the river animals safe into their lodges. It's nearly dark, and nothing is alive on the river. You may as well pull your traps, Trapper. The big one is always off on some other stretch of the river. Fat chance a pony-league trapper would ever trap the big one.

Out on the ice, you look up from the snow. Downstream, in the middle of the river, a dark hole in the ice interrupts the white. It looks like an open spot where the current is fast. Walking closer, eyes focused on the dark hole, you see it has girth. The hole in the ice is really a large dark mass. You approach the dark mass to within several feet before you realize what it is.

There on the ice, the old beaver sits, hunkered down, trapped. This is the one you've been after—you would catch him when you weren't looking. Isn't that how it goes. But what's he doing on top of the ice?

This is twice the animal you've ever trapped. Except it doesn't look like a beaver, more like a ragged skeleton with fur. Except it's alive. What's it doing out here?

During the big freeze the river level had dropped. You see now. The drown set, with the big killing Conibear, missed the head of the giant beaver and caught it over the back leg and tail. Still, the animal should have drowned. But the water was low. It climbed atop the boulder it was wired to and rested. The top of the boulder was only inches from the surface.

The beaver must have gotten caught days ago, before the freeze. Now it sits here, alive. Its back foot and tail are stuck in the trap, frozen in the ice. The animal can barely move. Only its body sways as you kneel before it. You can tell the animal is blind, the way it sways. It raises its head and sniffs the air, but seems to look past you. You're on your knees in front of the beaver, the cold seeping into your bones.

You see that the beaver has no teeth. It has chewed them down to the quick on the trap. The pelt is worthless, patchy and damaged. But my god it is big. Bigger than you've ever seen, and up close, worthless, but bigger than a dog, but worthless with its mottled pelt drooping on its bones.

The beaver hisses through its broken mouth. It coughs.

You have dispatched animals before, angry, gnashing their teeth, or near dead. The hulking beaver is diminished, but not nearly dead. You will kill it now with the sharp edge of the trapping tongs. There will be no more thunderous warning slaps of the tail, no more sharpening of teeth on big trees. You reach into your burlap sack for your trapping tongs, but they're not there. You should know better than leave your tools at home, Trapper. Now, you've got no tools for the job, but you've got the job still. You have just your trapping stick. You could walk home, nearly a mile, but it's almost dark.

You raise the heavy cane, feeling its familiar smoothness. Your first blow glances off the beaver's head. You hear only the heavy thud of the stick on the ice. The report echoes off downriver, then circles back. The vibration stings your hands. The beaver looks for an opponent, raising its head soundlessly. You raise the stick and strike the beaver again, accurately like you learned from hours of splitting wood. Blood spatters the snow. The beaver seems to curl within itself. No corner to back into, it backs into itself, head held high.

You strike again. The stick sounds heavily on the animal's skull. You strike again. Now the beaver has located you, through some other sense, and seems to look straight into you. You shorten your blows. Short blows save stamina. The raising of the stick is slow, and the falling swift. But now you feel something new. You feel the heavy stick crack near the end, and the deep thud becomes weaker. The new, weaker sound from the cracked stick echoes far off over the frozen river. This won't do. You've begun to sweat.

You stop, afraid suddenly that someone might be watching. You look around and up at the barren trees, swaying. You catch the scent of smoke.

Here you are on the frozen river in the gathering dark. It's too big. You can't finish. In the darkness the certain edges of daylight become wooly and strange. Soon, it won't even be your river. Soon, you'll be standing on a gravel road, or lost in a frozen field. Soon, the beaver will darken into tree, deeply knotted chunk of wood that needs splitting.

Heavy Machinery

The weather is not, like cosmology or the birth and death of stars, a remote system of hypothetical cataclysms describable only by the highest mathematics. It happens to us, it affects us. Therefore, the weather is in our heads as much as it is in the external world.

—*The Old Farmer's Almanac*, 2011

Her Blue Rabbit

Janet Worden's father Harlan is minced in the blades of the bush hog back in the south forty and her boyfriend Nick will have to bring in the dogs so they won't drag him up in parts. She has two fine wolfhounds and a spotted, flop-eared rabbit named after some German composer Nick can never remember. Janet never puts the rabbit down that early morning after she and Nick stumble into her house. Just sits there in the half-light on her piano bench and fingers the rabbit's face and irregular spots. Pastor Judy Homer is there and both their moms are there and Nick's still standing by the door thinking how unnatural it is that all the lights are on in the house but still it seems dark.

Janet's ma gives it to her straight. Dad was out on the tractor mowing weeds. He had an accident. The pastor breaks in and says they think it was a brain aneurism. He was probably gone before he ever got caught in the blades. A painless death. How else could you explain that happening to a veteran farmer? The pastor takes the two of them by the arm and tells them to be strong. Her hands are clammy just like they are when Nick shakes them before church every Sunday. Nick's ma says her old man's farming with God now.

Her ma tells Janet to round the dogs back up and put them in the basement. Janet mouths back and says it's stupid to bring them in with all the people. The two go back and forth. They sound just like they always do when they fight. Janet's fire comes from the absolute certainty that her mother is dead wrong, no matter what the issue. Her ma acts as if every snide reply is a pitchfork tine to the heart. Nick thinks maybe they have fallen back into that familiar territory to make all this seem normal.

Nick hasn't talked to Janet since four a.m. when he tried to drop her off in the driveway and she pitched a fit. There was Nick's ma standing on Janet's front porch in the middle of the night waving him in when the dogs burst out of the door behind her and sent her sprawling. Nick thought maybe he should pretend he didn't see her and drive home, but he noticed Janet standing there between his car and his ma, and she kept looking back and forth between them, like she was caught in his headlights, poor thing. Then he noticed the house lit up.

"Use your head, Janet," her ma is saying, her face stern and her coffee-stained teeth showing. "He's all over down there. The cops went back there to clean up, but the tractor kept running after..." Her voice trails off. But Janet doesn't get up from the piano bench and her fingers are stretched taught over the back of the rabbit, almost like she's trying to play the damn thing, and the rabbit looks like all it wants is to get the hell out of there.

So Nick gets up to let the hounds in and finds them jousting outside in the moonlit front yard, happy maybe that cars keep rolling into their territory. Animals. They don't have to outlast anything. The moon is high now and the low house, the ship of a barn and the row of molted oaks stand out in dark relief. Nick tells himself he needs to slow down, sort this out. He looks back in the direction of the south forty and gets some pictures in his head that he can't lose. Tractor's tipped into the culvert, popped out of gear. Her old man with his legs sticking out of the back of the bush hog, boots pointed down, like he's working on it only the PTO's still on. Her ma working her way down there towards the noise in the near-dark, wondering what the hell's going on, yelling first when she sees him and the tractor, then breaking into an odd run when she hears the blades still turning, a repeating thump. The dogs thinking it's a freaking hunt or something because she never runs, falling all over each other to get closest to her.

Nick wonders how close she is when she sees. Stop it. Jesus Christ. Maybe that's not how it happened. How should he know? It's October. The crops are in early. What the hell was old man Worden doing down there cutting weeds anyway?

He collars the hounds and budges them through the front door, but before he can shove them into the basement, they bust loose and gallop up the short landing and into the living room. They know what happens when there's company: lots of petting, cheek pulling, stick throwing, voices of praise. They stampede. Goddamn Chas still hasn't grown up and starts to pee from joy. His gray tail is like a scythe that mows a dish of her ma's homemade sweetmeats off the coffee table by the landing and they go skidding all down the stairs to where Nick's standing by the front door. Before anyone can stop the damn dogs, they're lapping up the sweetmeats, and her ma is lunging at their giant flanks. Janet, she's got this high-pitched voice, and she's screaming how her ma should have left the dogs outside, how it doesn't take that many brains, how her ma never did train the dogs. Her ma "oh Janeting" there behind the dogs while every tined remark sinks home. It's almost too much to take.

When they finally get the dogs put away it quiets down upstairs. Nick and Janet put their moms on the couch by the clammy-handed pastor. Nick's ma and the pastor comfort Janet's ma. There there. They put their hands all over her knees and shoulders—the formal places where hands always go—and they are all bawling. Nick's seen all this before. He knows what happens when the church people show up at your house in the middle of the night. Where hands go. Janet sees this and sloughs off invisible through a narrow doorway to the kitchen. Her straight blond hair blankets that stupid rabbit whose name Nick can never remember. It's her third damn rabbit; the wolfhounds keep thinking they're pull toys. Her old man keeps buying—kept buying—her new ones, each time warning, "Take care of this one." Nick finds himself alone in the living room with the adults. He avoids looking at them, slips two forgotten sweetmeats from the floor into his mouth in a cough gesture. Swallows. Picks a hair. Tiptoes. Goes pee. Keeps away from the water. Follows Janet.

"Jesus, he's fucking dead," she says when he finally makes it to the kitchen. She glances to the living room to see if she said it too loud. But the adults are safely away where they put them, out there on the edges of things.

"I'm sorry, Jan." Nick coughs from the food. Finally he can talk to her and he chokes. Shit. He hugs her then, but she's not wanting. She seems not to want to let this be her excuse, though he is willing to let it be.

"Are you drunk still?" she says to him. He doesn't know what to say to this. Really he's a puddle, but her old man's dead and he feels guilty. Nobody wants to be drunk when somebody dies. Their moms are out there too, the church, all this relationship hell. He thinks maybe he'll tell her he's not.

"I am, shit I'm glad I am," she says. She's got the bunny in a death grip up by her shoulder. Its split nose is twisting, maybe catching an air of radish. She almost laughs and her eyes are kind of frosty and then he notices that she hasn't even cried yet. Nick wonders if he should start crying, if maybe that would show her it's OK. He starts to make himself cry. He turns his back on her, blinks fast, thinks about weepy peaches, swallowyawns. Nothing doing. He reaches for the fridge instead, to pour them water. The pitcher is yellowed glass. He reaches for it blind, reaching for her, just misses. It breaks. His big dumb hands. There are potatoes and onions together in a wicker bowl by the fridge. Water everywhere. His skin itches.

"We're past curfew," she says to him and giggles, plays in the puddle. God this is unnatural.

When he picked her up earlier that night, Janet, her ma and old man were eating dinner. Old Man Worden was half in the bag already. Nick asked what's for dinner and that was his cue to say, "Bacon, eggs and potatas, cottage cheese and tomatas." Then he reached over and pinched her ma's ass. She dropped her fork. Nick didn't look. He knew she was humiliated. He'd seen it before. "Suey made my favorite," her old man said, mouth full. And he laughed at that and told Nick to have Janet home by three. He laughed again and they all laughed because they knew her curfew was midnight, but with Nick there was no curfew on account of their families being close. Those were the last words they ever heard from him. "Have her home by three." On the way out to the car, Janet made a point about how weird he was.

They stopped first by Shady Valley Quarry. It had been a week. Nick thought about bobber fishing. Then they got stinking drunk at the party. They poured their beer in shot glasses to get drunker. Drank it from straws. They fought a little. Nick said girls grow up to be their mothers. He flirted. Ruth got brave with Nick in the bathroom. Her eyes were spiders. He escaped unseen. All night he kept putting off talking to Janet. There were chairs at the party. They took turns sitting on each other. Nick felt like Janet deserved at least that.

On the way back home, he was all over the place. Janet even squealed once, though she was used to it. They stopped again at the quarry. This time it was work though. She cried like she knew it. Tears sobered Nick some. They drove home, parked. It was maybe four. He hadn't begun to tell her what he needed to when she rolled her window up and stepped out of the car. The guilty game. She was going to make him follow her. He decided to give her a head start when suddenly there was his ma. What was she doing there? Then the hounds. Ma's ass-over-tea-kettle. Janet a doe in the headlights. Nick, late.

Janet bends to pick a sharp leaf of glass off the wet linoleum. She feeds Flop a drink out of it. Nick wonders what she's thinking. He knows she thinks her old man's a bastard. Was a bastard. But that's gotta be over now. She's gotta be thinking now that he's all right. Was all right. Because really he was. Worden was a drunk. That's an old story. But he was a straight-ahead son-of-a-bitch. He would do these crazy-nice things. At Nick's graduation party in June her old man caught him by surprise with a hundred spot. Thing is, it was in this card that says Happy Anniversary Honey. Nick played dumb. They slammed a beer. Hell, nobody else gave him a hundred spot.

"I like this rabbit best," Nick tells Janet in the kitchen. She fiddles its whiskers with the glass, strums them. He fingers its nose. Their fingers wetly touch. Nick's thinking that "Have her home by three" is a lousy set of last words, and he won't get a chance to revise them. Then he thinks it's fine because he's sure her old man has different last words to everyone he knows. Some of them have to be better than his. He wonders what his last words to her ma are. She has last words too, he guesses, to her old man. So does Nick. And Janet. They all have last words. They don't go away either, so you must choose them carefully. Once you say them, you have them. In ten years he'll be saying, "My last words to her old man were. . ." *What were they?*

"What's his name again?" Nick's asking for it.

"Handel, dummy. I've told you a thousand times."

She stops there. Nick wants her to keep talking, to keep his mind from unwinding. She doesn't. She sidles up onto the counter, legs split, great legs. She's done that before. Stop it. Stop it. He can't believe her old man trusted him after what he did with his daughter on his kitchen counter.

"Don't wait up." Christ, what a lousy set of last words. He sure didn't, did he? Didn't bother to say goodnight. Stop it!

So now Nick will talk. Now Nick wants to say something right. Because they go way back, him and Janet. Her ma and his ma were friends even before that. Nick and Janet grew up a few miles away from each other on Hemlock Hollow Road, and he was friends with her for the lack of boys around. She started showing up at his house with her silly bike with the big basket in front and flowers painted on the seat, and that's just about the best thing Nick had going for him those days. They rode their bikes the five country miles around the block and even stopped underneath the old wooden bridge over Shady

River to check for dead possums. She was really cool about keeping her distance at school, so he wouldn't get ribbed by his other buddies. They grew up together. Later, all his pals got jealous because she bloomed into a looker. It all seemed natural, but the first time they did it, he fell off.

Nick knows Janet's story. The one he planned on telling her in soft terms that night in the driveway. It runs through his head here in the kitchen. Farm girl, tomboy, old friend. She likes fancy music. Can play anything on the piano. She gets pretty, actually kind of classy. Tomboy becomes comely neighbor girl with breasts Nick's friends are jealous over. Nick takes an interest. They're both curious. It happens fast, if awkwardly, he actually feels something, or was it just the explosion? Time passes. Trips to the quarry, the woods, the old wooden bridge. Has it been a year? It becomes edgeless. Habit. They grow up. Things change. There are other girls. There must be other boys? He misses the friendship. Can't they save that? They're changing. They can't deny that. Couldn't they be friends? Remember the good old times?

But now there's this with her old man. Two losses in one night is too much. It's time to back off, let her back if she'll let him. Comfort her. She deserves that. Say something right. Tell her something to make her laugh while there's still time, while this might still be just a bad joke, a play game. Here they are in the kitchen in a shambles, and she deserves to laugh. Dogs put away. Adults put away. Nick and Janet, obviously all night. Thinking about things they can't say. It has to be now because her life changes when she wakes up tomorrow. First just an empty spot at the breakfast table. Then empty places elsewhere.

Maybe he can tell her one about how funny she used to look with that big basket stuck to her bicycle. Sure. About how they grew up together and poked dead possums that were sometimes just pretending and dug around in her parents' underwear drawers and pilfered cigarettes from her old man, and beer. There are lots of funny, old-timey things he can talk about. About how he would doze on the couch during her music lessons, never knowing what she was doing, but liking the melody just the same. How if she started playing too much classical stuff he would tell her to play right. How they were friends. How one day when he came down to get some eggs for his ma she was barely dressed, it was so hot. And how he saw that she was beautiful. About how they went to the chicken coop together to gather eggs. How her hair was like the fresh straw in there. How he couldn't keep his hands off those warm eggs. How he grabbed for every last one, sweating. How they all got broken right there in the chicken coop when he lost his balance.

Instead she has one for him, and it takes him by surprise because he thinks he knows all her stories, has heard all this before.

"I used to wish for a blue rabbit," she tells him, and right away she's got his interest because he can tell it's going to be a happy story to make them laugh. Because that's how you deal with dark shit like this. Put it away somewhere. She goes on to say how her old man got her a blue rabbit when she was four. How he got a whole slew of baby rabbits to raise, but she could keep the blue one and it would be her special. How they kept all the rabbits out with the chickens in the chicken coop, except her blue one.

And this gets Nick thinking about the chicken coop and everything seems just right because this is the story he was going to tell. He's going to be in it. She goes on about how she loved that blue rabbit so much and carried it everywhere with her. How she carried it by its big floppy blue ears until there was no fur left on them. How, as the summer wore away, there always seemed to be fewer rabbits in the pen when she'd go to visit them, clutching her blue, sneaking a suck of her thumb. How it didn't really seem to matter because the rabbits and chickens were so much alike, such friends, so soft and white together. How it never dawned on her until every last rabbit but her blue was gone. And how at first she thought the white rabbits just grew beaks and feathers and became white chickens.

And how it struck her when she found a stray white puff on this same yellowed kitchen linoleum, a red stem. How clear it became. And how her mother finally confessed the thing she had done early mornings while Janet slept. And how Janet swore she would never eat the rabbits. And how her mother told her it was too late. How she'd been eating rabbit all along in casseroles. And how mad Janet was. But how good the rabbit tasted. How sweet.

And how time made her forget that. How she learned later how to butcher rabbits. How to hold a rabbit by the head with one hand and by the shoulder with the other and just give a little pull. And how it was just as easy as that. How you could do it right in the cage with the other rabbits and how they just never caught on. How they sniffed the air with their split noses and hopped right up to you, even as you were making a stack of them. And how they stiffened right away. How to hang them by their lucky little feet and do the rest with the knife.

And how her blue died, finally, left hiding in the weeds her old man took the bush hog to.

This she tells Nick, when he thought he knew her story.

Amuck, The Great Engine

Heck drives a train. Has for forty years and here's Mister Railroad Examiner telling him he's made his last run. Heck's heard all this before. Heck hauls freight for the Burlington Northern and has been up and down the line a few times.

Did you even see her? Examiner asks Heck. Did you see her in that vintage Caddy nosed out on the track? Or were you having yourself a little siesta? God that red Caddy must have been shining like the fucking sun. A five thousand dollar paint job. Did you apply the brake when you first saw her? Did you pull the whistle? You seem to be a magnet for death, Heck. This time you're at the end of the line.

He is badgering, but Heck knows that's just part of the inquest. They try to rattle you until you admit you were asleep, drunk or somehow liable. Heck doesn't rattle. Heck says calmly that he applied the handbrake when he saw the nose of the red Cadillac out across the track. He gives the statistics correctly: how he was going fifty and how he was hauling sixty freight cars with three engines and how long it would take a freight train to stop with all that weight behind her. How he laid on the horn and everything. Heck knows he is innocent by a good fifty yards, and he will be cleared, again. He hasn't just fallen off the coal car, after all.

There is basically no suspense. Heck is back on the job in no time. But here it is splashed about the papers and even on the TV news and everyone is interested in Heck's job again. Now everyone is interested in trains. Trains. Trains. Trains. Heck barely gets back to work after a paid week off and here's Channel 12 from Milwaukee doing a ride along and asking all sorts of questions about what life is like as an engineer:

Channel 12: Heck. Now there's an interesting name. How did you end up with a name like Heck?

Heck: What's that?

Channel 12: I said your name. It's rather peculiar. How did you get it?

Heck: It's a nickname.

Channel 12: OK. We won't pry. How about your life on the rails? We understand you got your start shoveling coal for the steam locomotives in the 50s. That must've been hard work. What can you tell us about those difficult early days?

Heck: Wasn't too tough hauling my paycheck home Fridays.

Channel 12: Okay. Well. What about now? What's it like to spend these long hours in a locomotive?

Heck: Wanna drive?

Channel 12: No. I'd better not, thank you. This seems like a peaceful profession. Do you find solitude out here on the rails?

Heck: What's that?

Channel 12: I said solitude. Do you find it driving trains?

Heck: Sometimes I'll find asparagus, sometimes venison, a pheasant. The wife packs me a lunch. Otherwise I'll find a beanery.

Channel 12: Okay. So. Issues. What do you think of the national trend to dismantle the rails? Seems it's cheaper to ship by semi and travel by bus. Any thoughts on that?

Heck: Nope. Never driven a bus. Trains don't get flat tires.

Channel 12: Seems you're a man who likes to cut to the chase, so I'll cut to the chase. Do you feel responsible when someone dies at your hands?

Heck: What's that?

Channel 12: I said have you ever killed a person.

Heck: What's that?

The boys at the round house all give Heck a slap on the back after the Channel 12 News. Way to tell 'em Heck, they say, and other things with smiles Heck doesn't quite hear. Occasionally, there are smirks, giggles. Really, Heck is sick of all the attention. He wants people to let him be. Usually it's only the hobbyists asking him silly questions about such-and-such model number, and such-and-such old depot. Now everyone wants to ride with Heck and hear about the latest accident. Even his wife wants to know about this woman with the fancy red car and fur coat, even his kids. So Heck tells them to read the paper. Says there is really nothing more to it than the paper says. At night in bed Heck's wife is a snoring lump next to him, and Heck lies awake late listening.

Heck has read the paper himself, and it even says how he is innocent. The paper even says how it was the woman's fault and how it usually is the fault of the person who is in too much of a hurry to wait for the train. How people think they can beat the trains. This woman, though, didn't want to scratch her Cadillac. The man who pulled up behind her told the story to the newspaper, and the railroad has his whole excited account recorded for the investigation.

She was wearing a fur coat, the man says on the tape recording. I saw the whole thing. She pulled too close to the tracks and the cross bar came down on the hood of the vintage Caddy. When she didn't get out, I went up to her car. It was this gorgeous candy apple with tail fins—I'd say it was a '59—and she had this gorgeous mink. Strictly class. I say, 'Lady, you better back it up. That train's bearing down.' She tells me I'm crazy if I think she's gonna back up and scratch her Caddy. This baby has got five grand just in paint, she says. She just had it restored. I guess I can see how she felt because her paint is worth more than my whole car.

Anyway, she tells me I better lift the cross bar up off her hood and then she'll back up. So I try. I'm strong and I try. I go tug on the thing, but it's locked and the train's bearing down. All spotlight, thunder and whistle. You know, just like in the movies. So I go tell the lady to back it up and she refuses. Says, get this, the train will stop for her. Like she's holy water or something. So I can tell she's nuts, and I'm gonna yank her outta there. I try to reach in the window and open her door, which is locked, but she rolls the window up, and I get my fingers stuck. You know, right across the fingernails. Smarts city. So I yank them out and they're killing and I back off because here comes the train.

She must see it's not gonna stop because pretty soon she starts to panic. I see her struggling with her seatbelt. She finally gets it off and decides just to get out of the car. So she gets out, just as the train is coming into the picture. She's got these high heels that match her car, and she's got legs, too. And she's gonna make it. She even reaches in to grab her purse and she's gonna make it. Except—and this is the part I can't fucking believe—she turns around to shut the fucking door, and her fucking mink gets stuck right the fuck in it. No shit, and I see her look out at me and now she's all white. Man oh man. Her mink was even scared white. And I'm on my knees back on the road screaming, 'Fucking move. Fucking move! Fuck the Caddy, move!' But it's too late. She's trying to get out of the mink, but it's like stuck to her. I see her heels click once and then it comes. Whammo! She goes flying with the car. She goes right fucking along with the Cadillac. I saw the whole thing. The train like ate the whole car and everything.

No kidding, I was just finishing my lunch break and maybe that's why I thought of it like that, but that's what I saw. The train ate her. And it was her seatbelt that did it. I'm never wearing mine again. It was her seatbelt and that damn mink. And the 5K paint job too. Man, I never loved my junker more. And that gorgeous Caddy. I don't know why she pulled so close. Man oh man, the train swallowed her right the fuck up."

Heck has heard this recording, and he feels comfortable about his job. He's back where he belongs, thanks in part to this rummy. Heck's not at the end of the line, not by a long shot. Except he doesn't feel quite right. The trains have these complicated new radios for calling ahead to the switch men and line crew. They have too many goddamn knobs, Heck thinks. And, too, with all the cutbacks, Heck doesn't have a brakeman to ride along with him anymore. Here they can afford all this digital defugalty but no brakeman. Now it's all the time Heck alone in the engine with the complicated gadgets.

And sometimes Heck gets sleepy around noontime. Sometimes he's scared to be there, and sometimes he's scared he has forgotten how to operate this locomotive. It often feels like it's barreling along down the track without him. And he can feel all those cars lined up back there pushing him down the track, and he can't do anything to stop it. But he knows that can't be because he has operated these trains for forty years. He can drive them in his sleep. He wonders sometimes if it's his fault when someone gets in the way of his train. And he wonders what will happen to him for running down all those people. How many has it been? A dozen? Surely less than that.

Heck remembers the first one and all the guilt he felt. Here was this old man running alongside the tracks. This was out past Bergamot Pond and this little hunched-over man was running along the tracks on the cinders. Heck was a new engineer, just married, and no one even called him Heck back then, and here was this little old man along the tracks who never even looked at the train, just turned smack into it. Made a left turn just as the train came, just as if the train was a magnet as Mister Examiner said. The locomotive just bumped the old man, and he only bounced a few yards, but when Heck finally brought the big load to a halt and went back to check, the old man was dead. He must've been eighty. And he was barefoot. Heck looked around for the old man's boots, but he couldn't find them anywhere.

And then there were the newlyweds a few years later. Their newlywed car stretched with newlywed streamers and balloons shot out of nowhere and Heck smashed it all to hell. And all the love and happiness newlywed streamers got draped across the engine and Heck couldn't see out his windshield for all the joy. Heck wondered with Evelyn what he should do. Should he attend the funeral? Should he send letters of condolence to the families? Flowers? Maybe he should start going to church with Evelyn. Would the families of the newlyweds think he was a murderer? Was he a murderer?

In the end, Heck just waited out the time of each investigation and went back to work. He sent no flowers, attended no funerals and prayed at no church. In the end he was just too embarrassed. Heck felt that maybe everyone would sooner forget if he just stayed in his train. Heck did say some prayers on his train though. He said them to God that he was sorry about running over the new couple and could God please help him forget about it now. He prayed a lot like that early on and pretty soon he did stop seeing the car with the streamers come out of nowhere and mostly he did forget about it. Mostly he forgot about it all the way up until the time when the little boy on his bike came out of nowhere too. He pedaled along barefoot with a stringer of carp draped across the handlebars. Except Heck didn't pray to forget this time because he forgot to thank God when he had his first prayer answered. He forgot to say thank you so he was too embarrassed to pray to God again and remind him. But Heck mostly forgot about the boy with his fish too. Pretty soon he could get back to work without God's help. And he slept most nights.

Heck thinks about these things as he rolls across Iowa and Wisconsin in his train. Now he can't seem to forget anything. Heck is gone three days at a time and he spends his nights in the same motels. He carries his same grip and eats at the same beaneries. All the faces of the crew are smiling and familiar when Heck goes to the roundhouse in the morning, and Heck thinks that everything will again be okay. When he drives his train past Shady Valley Feed and Grain, he hangs his arm out the window at the crossings and people wave at him like they always do, and he waves back in a long, arching wave. And Heck doesn't mind being friendly to people when they're in their cars and he's in his train. Heck doesn't really mind that people love his train.

Heck thinks too that maybe there is a good reason for all the deaths he's responsible for. He is responsible for them, finally. But as Evelyn said, maybe there was a positive purpose for each. How about the little boy? He died in innocence, his stringer full. And that old man, that first one, was an old, old man. Evelyn helped Heck think that maybe there are worse ways to go than how that old man went. No shoes on. No suffering. Just a soft bump toward death. And the newlyweds. Evelyn reasoned that they died in ecstasy, or imagining ecstasy.

Remember our wedding night? Evelyn had said. Remember how happy we were? Maybe, she helped him believe, it wouldn't be so bad to go in a moment like that. Maybe their souls would be that happy forever.

But Evelyn isn't always here to help Heck be positive. No, she isn't. Mostly, he is alone in his thundering digital engine that seems to be almost beyond his control. Anyway, Evelyn makes it seem like everyone is better off being dead. Like everyone is lucky that Heck comes along in his big train and plows them down. What about this woman in her shining red chariot? Was there a reason for her? Heck thinks maybe God was mad at this woman for something she did. That's what Evelyn would say. Maybe God was mad because she was so rich and worried about material things. Mister Examiner had said Heck was a magnet for death. Maybe that was so. Maybe

God used him to kill the selfish woman. Maybe, Heck thinks, just maybe he is the engine of God.

Heck thinks about the accident and how it happened. About the story the newspaper didn't know. He remembers there was a straight stretch of track and how he was comfortable after eating the liverwurst sandwich with pickle Evelyn had packed which he had warmed up on the sideboard heater like always. And the sandwich was delicious and there would be no switches coming for tens of miles and Heck wouldn't have to fool with the radio. He was comfortable and it was a sunny day and the long train was very much in control. Heck could just drive and drive. He remembers kicking his boots off, propping his feet on the dashboard and resting his left hand on the shiny metal handbrake. Comfortable for a while. The roar of the engine was long since a shock to his ears. This loud thunder had become a reassuring strum. Heck burped a liver flavor and relaxed.

The train rocked gently on the uneven tracks. It careened away across the countryside, lullaby-like, forward and then back again. The train stretched in the belly until it was a great stringer of cars on straight track that stretched all the way across the Middle West as a girdle, holding the country in check. And there, up front and spry in striped bibs and railroad cap, was a young and alert Heck at the helm. Humming, humming, happy at his new job of engineer. His new wife. Happy at the nickname his father gave him. 'A rambling wreck from Georgia Tech,' his old man would sing, 'and a heck of an engineer.' That was it, the young Heck thought proudly, waving in long arches at every car at every crossing. A heck of an engineer. Made for this momentous job. Heck was he.

And suddenly there was something shining in the tracks. At first just a shining red sunrise. Peaceful. A beacon. A shining ambition Heck was headed for. But the bright red became an interruption in the seamless track ahead. Heck found his hand, old again, on the brake lever, and he turned it. His feet shot down to the floor of the engine and he sat erect. He saw then, from perhaps a half mile away, that it was no sunspot. And he knew already it was much too late. All he could do was watch as the bright red object got closer. A slow-motion event. Heck looked around but there was no one in the engine with him. He was alone and the red blur was becoming a car. It was becoming larger. The train was slowing, but not nearly enough. And soon, through the glare of red, Heck saw a person. A man struggling with the cross bar.

Heck began to sweat as he had on these occasions before. He sat helplessly in his seat and waited for this to happen. He saw a man struggling by the driver's side door of the car. Heck saw him retreat, saw a car door open. It became the door of a Cadillac, but this was a vehicle from another time. Heck saw a woman whose coat shone in the sun. And Heck tried to be a veteran engineer who had seen many potential fatalities pass by in a harmless blur. His tongue passed over his lower lip once, again. Heck braced for the impact and waited for the woman to move. She seemed stuck to her car. Then, the car and the woman disappeared beneath his view. The impact was no soft bump. It was a resounding percussion that shot Heck up out of his seat. The impact was a culmination of all those earlier collisions, and for a moment Heck didn't know where he was nor how old. When he came to his senses, he saw his boots were off. He thought for a moment he had been knocked out of them.

Bird Watching

The earth is now rapidly ripening her fruits and seeds of all kinds, the leaves on the elm begin to change their colour, the young starlings begin to congregate in flocks, the golden sparwort and the sunflower are in bloom, the poisonous berries of the deadly nightshade ripen, meteors abound in the atmosphere.

—*The Farmer's Almanac and Calendar*, 1841

Unlovely Night at the Wooden Nickel

Like most people who find some arbitrary numerical constructions with which to chart the slow decline of their lives, decades say, I've come to measure my descent in women, and since I can never keep a woman around for a year let alone a decade, the sad litany of my life I measure in months. I am a serial lover, faithful to each for her time. And I think it's best this way, until end game again, when I review the litany, amazed by the heart's ability to withstand punishment, to pump itself clean, but unsure, too, if it will work this time. Wednesday finds me at the Nickel a day early, drinking a left-handed beer and mourning Monique, soon to be latest gone, by recalling her predecessors.

Twenty-four months ago it was Rhonda, who, being armless from birth, could perform almost any function with her feet. She could sit up at the bar and drink a glass of Red Label with her feet and smoke cigarettes with her toes, bringing the lit cigarette to her lips as casually with her right foot as I could with my left hand. More, she rolled her own, and could pinch the tobacco and roll a perfect weed all the while sitting up there at the bar and talking dirty things to you, if that's what you liked. She could even shoot a fair pool game if you propped her up. I loved Rhonda for a while and we had quite a time, for a good eight months, having lots in common besides just beer and cigarettes, which we both cared for dearly. She could drive straight too, feet at ten and two, and it was many Thursdays she drove us home in her sturdy old Buick while I passed out in the seat beside.

Then there were the brief, sweet four months of Ruth. She was a singer and Great Lakes swimmer. She hooked me when she told me how the wind across the plains had a very under water quality, how when you're under water in the lake and an outboard wings by, you can hear the whine of the outboard, like wind. She was right about that. I'm a sucker for a smart broad, and I told her that was the best idea I'd heard for weeks, which was true. Ruth began to sing karaoke Thursdays at the Nickel. She could pull out her two front teeth and sing other people's songs as if they were actually her own. I couldn't hold a note to save my life, and that was a sore spot from the start.

You're tone deaf, she told me.

We make silent music, I told her, arguing what I'd read about the music of the spheres, how bodies make music just moving through the void oblivious of one another. We could be making a beautiful waltz right now, I sang, and twirled convincingly across the sawdust floor. But she was gone even then. She left me eventually for a hair-lipped blacksmith named Wetnight who did, her words, a heart-rending *Lonesome Town*. The thing is, people come into your life, but they never really go out, despite what you do to grind down their memories small. I'll never see Ruth again, though her impression's here yet. Sometimes I see it on the bed sheets and elsewhere. Every place she was seems to mourn the loss of her.

For better or worse, though, Unlovely Night at the Wooden Nickel seems to offer a bottomless well of damaged goods and deformities. Thursday's clarion call is heard halfway across Odette County and there doesn't have to be a week in the year when you endure your damage alone. You get to feeling so low during the week, but it seems that the Wooden Nickel has something for every case.

And so it happens that I'm already headlong into the months of Monique before the last month of Ruth had run its sorry course. I tell you I'm not obsessed with cosmetic beauty and that might explain why I would date Monique, who has, her words, a bit of a hunchback. But despite the hunchback, or perhaps because of it, Monique is a beautiful woman. I kid you not. And one hell of an athlete. She's a tennis player and a regular pro about it. Plays on a club team at The Groves, and Sundays I motor in to watch her. She moves over the court like a deer, and you can't hardly feel sorry for her at all. I think part of her endowment is that her opponents do feel sorry for her at first. I mean, the first time you see her, she does look pitiable, like she couldn't possibly be any good with her shoulder jutting upward like some horn trying to erupt from her back. At first blush you think she's on the team because of some souvenir rule about cripples. But this hunchback girl Monique—beautiful name for a girl—her parents must have given her that name to compensate, like some ornithologist who gave that ugly brown bird the beautiful name, starling. Say it. Star-ling. Anyway, Monique, she's beautiful out there. Mo-nique. And it's a pleasure to watch her and the looks on the faces of her opponents as they're being out pointed by a hunchback. So much of tennis is about being beautiful in the usual cosmetic sort of way. I guess it's not just tennis.

People are always feeling sorry for other people for the wrong reasons, and it costs them.

In bed she's no slouch either. I suppose you're already imagining that. She isn't exceptional in the grotesque Penthouse Forum sort of way. She's just graceful and, well, exotic, you know, and you can't help smiling all the while. I think what I love about her the most is her smile. It's an awfully crooked thing, but it's crooked in the opposite way that her back is crooked, so that, compositionally, everything evens out, and when you're with her, you forget she's a hunchback at all, except in public when everyone's staring at you.

The months of Monique. They've come to nearly twelve, my longest stint by a long way. But I can feel them slipping away even as they're happening. My life tends to occur this way, a somewhat dreary game of gain and loss. Love, love. Fifteen-love. Thirty-love. Last week, after her match—it was a chilly day—she made a cruel comment about my stump, about the purplish color of it. I only have one arm, the left, and I'm pretty sensitive about the right being gone, as you might expect. I mean, I never bring it up. Who likes to be defined by what they don't have? I also don't want sympathy. Already you're letting me off the hook because I'm a one-armed guy, but I'll warn you, I've learned to use the lack to my advantage. All the unlovelies learn this trick, and it keeps us in the game, so watch out.

Anyway, it started with the stump. A slight imperfection that had gone mostly unmentioned until then. This is an important moment for all of us, when a love-object begins to blemish, become mere object. I can understand her feeling. The thing is, I've looked at beauty. I've seen it in her for christ's sake. She must have seen it in me, fleetingly. What is she supposed to do, forget it? Surely she knows how quickly it can slither back into its hole, the damp earthworm, beauty.

So this is how it goes: that night in bed, in the dark, after another miracle, I feel her finger tracing the geography of my face. And it isn't moving there out of love and caress. I feel it pause when it finds a lack or glut. Not enough chin, too much lip. Her moist finger probes my mouth and finds a clump of tongue that's softer than most, an overbite. She finds my whole body a morass of dents and hollows, so many comings and goings. How can it be the same after she discovers this? We lie there petrified. In the morning, or some morning soon, she'll be gone, and I'll be alone again, a half of something.

It's Wednesday night at the Wooden Nickel. A dead night. Old One Nut pours me a freebie. He knows I'm low, so he offers his hillbilly discourse on the sublime and the beautiful, but I'm not taking. My mind's on Monique. She's a goner for sure. And I wonder will I be able to crush down the memory of her to make room for more. And I wonder, too, if all the incompletions make somehow for a life.

It is some comfort to be here. There is the old stuffed musky above the bar and the jackalope to catch out the foreigners. The bartop is no great shakes: a long brown thing, dented and used, but sturdy, and the line of three-legged stools seems to carry on forever. I think about all the Wooden Nickels stitched in a crooked pattern across the fat belly of the country, holding the country together, holding the guts in. The lovelies come in here and see guys like me crapped out on barstools and they think, dismal resignation. But that's not right. Tomorrow night is Unlovely Night at the Wooden Nickel and I'll have my boots on. There's tonight to get through though, and Monique. Monique. Already I can feel the lack of her. It comes as a tingle where her protrusion would fit up under my stump just so.

Down
Shady River

The hecklers came down river in rafts. There were four of them—boys from town—and they came down river drinking beer and raising hell. They tied their rubber rafts together to form a flotilla and barged right down the throat of the sluggish little river. Now they floated by the Purifoy house and were adrift in the eddy caused by the wing dam Mr. Purifoy had built with his own two hands. They idled around there in the deep catfish water surrounded by a flotsam of empties. The boys began filling beer cans with river water and launching them. Mrs. Purifoy was up on the berm grubbing in her hostas when she heard the commotion. She looked up just as the first of the beer grenades came barging in on her backyard solitude.

The sloped, earthen berm behind the Purifoy house rose up a good fifty yards from the river. There was a row of sandbags three high along the top of the ten-foot berm, left over from last year's flood. Now, even with the water back where it belonged, Mr. and Mrs. Purifoy lived with the sudden possibility that it could rage out of control at any time. So they left the sand bags in place. But Mrs. Purifoy had planted hostas along the inside of the sandbags, so their home seemed less a war zone.

From atop the berm, behind the sandbags, Mrs. Purifoy couldn't see the faces of the boys for the willow branches along the water's edge. She wasn't alarmed really. It wasn't uncommon for townies to come carping down her river on weekends. Usually, they put their rafts or canoes in at the Main Street Bridge in town, eight miles upriver, and took out at the old wooden bridge near her house. Neither was it uncommon for the townies to scatter their garbage around the river banks. She was prepared to ignore them. Easier just to clean up the mess after the drunken litterbugs had floated off. This was her attitude now: let be. She wouldn't even bother Mr. Purifoy, who was either up looking at the ball game or out working in his vegetables. But then the jeers started hurtling toward her along with the beer grenades.

"That you, Lila?" one of the boys hollered. "You got some thirsty boys down here wanna taste somma your sweet strawberry lemonade. Quit grazin' on them weeds and bring us some on down."

Lila Purifoy thought she recognized the voice, even for the forced southern drawl, and any doubts were erased when she saw through the willow branches the red and white welder's cap one of the boys was wearing. Then she knew who she was dealing with. Lila dropped her spade. She crouched and peered over the sandbags at her nemesis.

"Peekaboo Lila!" called a boy named Nathan Heller, known half across Odette County by the nickname Boney. She didn't recognize the other boys and guessed that Boney must have recruited them from Bergamot or some other town. Boney was her Carmen's latest ex, more jetsam created by her youngest daughter's ferocious appetite for, but purely miserable taste in boys. Boney was three years out of Shady Valley High, but he didn't act it. He worked part-time trucking for Shady Valley

Feed and Grain and spent his nickels on the high school girls. He was a seedy character, that Boney Heller, and her Carmen took to him like a duck to a June bug. Why was anybody's guess, but that she was a sucker for a hangdog look. He wore that filthy old polka-dotted skull cap and chewed snuff, and it made Mrs. Purifoy sick, just sick, to see her pretty Carmen glom onto him like she did, sniffing around in his mangy, pot-smelling hair and always sitting smack on top of him.

Boney had roared into their driveway in his broken-down jalopy one day during Carmen's junior year and caused a ruckus in their lives ever since. But her Carmen finally kicked him to the curb when she graduated a month earlier. She moved out almost immediately after, and took up with a flock of other fast girls, said she wanted to rid herself of all that restricted her. It sure was quiet around the house with her Carmen gone and no more Boney Heller sniffing around. But now a newly-rejected Boney was roaring again down by the river.

"Come down here Lila and talk to us fishy boys," Boney yelled, struggling to maintain his accent. He was standing up in his tipsy raft. His friends were holding onto his legs to support him, and he held a can of beer in each hand. "We want to talk about sweet Carmen's strawberry bottom. She shows everyone her ripe strawberry bottom, don't she boys?" His friends were laughing and hollering, slapping their paddles on the water like beavers warning danger. They were making an awful racket.

Mrs. Purifoy was weak. She said so herself there on the berm, kneeling in the bushy flowers. Just weak. She had been strong. She raised three daughters up well by her and Mr. Purifoy's good example. But Carmen had been her undoing. Yes, she was weak, and sick too. She felt as though she couldn't even raise up off her knees to face the boys—they were only boys after all—and that Boney was a skinny, dopey-looking boy. Why, only three or four years ago she would have taken a broom to such a cobbled-up troop of dirty boys and whisked their filthy mouths and faces right away from her. Seventeen years driving the school bus for Shady Valley District, she knew a few things about scallywags. But these boys were more brazen. What business did they have coming down her river and slopping up her yard?

Mrs. Purifoy looked around. Except for the sandbags, everything was as it should be. Her flowers were in full bloom in nice rows all along the berm and in the square bed over the septic tank. There around the birdbath was a circle of brilliant orange poppies that blossomed just so. Look, there was a little chipmunk scurrying along, and all the pretty songbirds were visiting her bird feeder there at the other end of the hill. There were chickadees and titmice and purple finches flitting. And oh, here comes Mrs. Grosbeak for a late bath after tidying up the nest. Doesn't she look fine?

Then an ugly black grackle flew up to the feeder and began scattering seeds. Mrs. Purifoy started. "Scat!" she told the bird, who paid her no never mind. "Scat!" She would have to get Mr. Purifoy to shoot that ugly damned bird. He was still a good eye with the pellet gun.

"Li-la...Li-la...I see you."

Mrs. Purifoy was startled again at the sound of her name. She barely recognized her own name spoken like that—with syrup poured all over it. She had forgotten about the boys for a moment and thought maybe they had just drifted away. Out of beer-can ammunition, the boys were all quiet now, except for Boney, who was getting louder and more brash.

"Lila! Quit fuckin' in them weeds. Come down river here and let old Boney plant his little flower where he likes to plant it. I promise I'll plant it real good in the loamy loam loam. I'll water it regular."

Mrs. Purifoy blanched. The black grackle purpled. The songbirds took soundless flight. She felt dizzy there under the late morning sun, weak. "Trouble," she murmured. She had been sitting up on her knees, but now she lumbered heavily onto all fours, and her head swung in among the bushy plants. "Dad!" she yelled out weakly. "Trouble, Dad. We got trouble Dad, down here by the river."

Mr. Purifoy was in the front yard hoeing in his vegetables when he heard his wife yell weakly something about trouble. He wasn't hearing too good these days after all those years in noisy milk trucks and noisy milk houses with loud machines blaring. Even though he was retired from his milk route now, he still heard a ringing in his ears that sounded just like he was at work all day. "I'm deaf in one ear and can't hear out of the other," he would always say. To tell the truth, it was nice to be hard of hearing sometimes, and sometimes he played more deaf than he was to avoid listening to his wife or his one daughter. One ear was nearly useless, however, and when his wild daughter blasted her cockamamie music, he would roll over in bed and turn his deaf ear to the whole tumultuous business. He was old and tired, and that way he could sleep.

Trouble. Something about trouble. Probably she was worried again about some black bird gobbling up all her precious bird seed, reigning terror on all the songbirds. He sure was tired of shooting at those black birds. He couldn't hit them anymore anyway, on account of his equilibrium was off, and they just taunted him, lifting a mocking wing to let the errant pellet pass by. Sometimes he ended up nailing one of the pretty songbirds. Then he'd have to sneak around until he had a chance to collect the dead little tuft and send it off down river before his wife found out. Some trouble all right. He had enough to worry about here in the garden. He just wanted to finish up hoeing in the beans, so he could go look at the ball game.

His garden was in good shape, he thought, stretching his aching back, looking over the nice straight rows of beans, carrots, beets and sweet corn. It was in good shape because he cultivated the soil and dug out all the rocks. He carried water in five gallon buckets from the river, and he carried horse manure in the same buckets from the neighbor's barn. He even kept the rabbits out with chicken wire. And if any weeds or volunteers shot up where he didn't want them, he'd hack them out with his hoe. He did this work because he knew it would pay off in a nice crop. Too bad his hard work in other areas didn't pay off so well. Things were getting so it didn't matter much what you did. Maybe there was such a thing as a bad seed, he thought. He finished up with the hoe and headed in to check the game. First, though, he guessed he'd better go see what the trouble was this time.

When Mr. Purifoy rounded the house to where he could see the river, he lost his balance and braced himself against the house. There was Lila flat on her stomach on the berm. What the hell was she doing? Then he saw the rafts out in the river, the beer cans in the yard, boys clambering like salamanders onto his wing dam. The red welder's cap. "What's going on Lila?" he yelled, and his wife rolled over to face him. He saw a blank look of confusion and fear in her eyes.

"Li-la..." Boney called, excited. "Would you look who's here. Here comes the milkman, Lila. Here comes the milktoast wants somma that sweet strawberry milk."

Mr. Purifoy flushed. He clenched his fists, gritted his teeth. It was that goddamn Boney. He would have to take that goddamn Boney clan and knock their goddamn heads together once and for all. He would take them by their long goddamn hair and throw their skinny white bread into the goddamn river. He'd done it enough before. Peeping Toms. Unwanted Johns. Fresh Billy Bobs. He'd taken all the ignorant bastards and knocked their ignorant goddamn heads together all these years, and he'd do it again. He'd do it again this time, and they wouldn't come around no more.

Mr. Purifoy ran for his wife, but in the first few steps felt dizzy and stumbled. The short span to the top of the berm seemed to stretch out in a long, wobbly mine field in front of him. There was a buzzing in his ears, and he imagined then that he was back in the war and making for a fox hole under sniper fire. When he finally reached the sandbags, he stumbled to the ground next to his fellow infantryman and rolled over. When he looked up, he was lying in the flowers with his wife. He was flat on his back.

"We're not comin' up there, Mr. and Mrs. Milktoast," Boney cajoled. "You're comin' down here." Mr. Purifoy rolled over to peer above the sandbags, and pointed his good ear downhill. His wife held him tight. Boney and the other boys were still on the wing dam, their rafts pulled ashore. They had begun to throw the large rocks from the wing dam back into the river, causing ruination.

Boney sang out loud and clear, "We got every right to be on this here Shady River, Milktoast. You don't own it. And we got every right to dismantle this here dam. Do we got a right, boys? Yeah, we got a right. You're the one don't got a right. You don't got a right to dam up something what runs its own course. You catch my drift, Milktoast? Now come down here! We're not gonna muddy no water you come down here nice."

The nerve. Where did that rumdum Boney get the nerve? Mr. Purifoy would be dipped in shit. He would have to take care of that knot-headed rumdum once and for all. But the potency of Boney's words seemed to take the fight right out of him, just as it had his wife. The nerve: Mr. Purifoy knew where the boy had got it. He himself had let this lawlessness go on too long, and now Boney figured he had the upper hand. Now Mr. Purifoy had lost it.

That was the shooting match. Mr. Purifoy's days of head knocking were over. Who was he kidding? He was just a clumsy old man trying to hang on to his rocker. The whole goddamn world had gone to blooey, and he'd gone right on to blooey with it. He rolled over and groped for his wife. Mrs. Purifoy seemed to sense his despair. She felt it too, what had gone wrong. She felt the burden of blame fell on her shoulders, that she had brought this pox upon them.

Lila Purifoy never shut the bathroom door. All these years there had never been any closed doors in her house. She raised three daughters up right, to be honest and open, but she kept an eagle eye out all the same. She even went so far as to give up her privacy in the bathroom, so she could be watchful. This method worked. Her oldest three had grown up and married respectable, each moving to Midwestern cities. But with Carmen, who had come along much later—an accident, a blessing—she softened.

With sweet little Carmen, candy apple of her daddy's eye, she closed the bathroom door. And her Carmen ran amuck. By the time Carmen was a loud-mouthed teen, all hell broke loose. Mrs. Purifoy got tired of shouting rules over the drone of derelict music. Curfew evaporated.

Their house had a revolving door, and Mr. and Mrs. Purifoy were the doormats. Mr. Purifoy had turned his deaf ear on the matter, said he was no longer savvy to the bafflement of youth. Lila, like always, should handle all business with the wooden spoon, and he'd be there to back her up. This method too, had worked in the past. But these days it was getting so it no longer mattered what you did.

Then their beautiful daughter started going with bad boys. She would bring them around the house and drape herself all over them just to spite her mother. She wore indecent clothes and bruises in a necklace. When she was just fifteen, she went with a grease monkey who was already out of school. He had the dirtiest grease monkey fingernails Mrs. Purifoy had ever seen, and it made her just ill to think of those hands on her daughter. He was polite, but dumb as a stump, and even though Mr. Purifoy called him a goddamn ignorant bastard right to his face, he kept showing up on their doorstep like some whupped hound.

Then one day Mrs. Purifoy caught Carmen and the grease monkey together in the bathroom with their tongues out. Carmen was on the pedestal sink, and the grease monkey's dirty hands were nowhere to be seen. That was it. Her daughter had finally gone too far. Mrs. Purifoy rose up to reclaim her household. Later that day, she sat her daughter down on the toilet and took a dull scissors to that beautiful head of strawberry blond locks. As if to prove it made no difference, Carmen let her. When she was done cutting, Mrs. Purifoy made her daughter look in the mirror. "Do you see yourself?" she said triumphantly. "You're a boy now. Other boys will have nothing to do with you."

But of course they did. And of course it was too late, and of course Carmen was already well beyond the reach of Lila's motherly wing. And next came Boney Heller and the sad litany of this last year when all boundaries were crossed, all taboos broken and all remnants of respectability torn down and trod upon in a muck-muck of remorse. Her Carmen was now a woman of the world, and a sad old pair of cowbirds sat alone on an empty nest.

Mr. Purifoy was the first to stand up from behind the sandbags and brush the dirt from his clothes. He had come to his senses. He lent a hand to his wife, and they stood up together, dirty and rumpled, leaning on each other for support. "We'll go talk to that rabble of hootniks," he said, basking in his moment of clarity. "We'll go talk to them, and they'll leave us be because they're people like you and me. That Boney's not the world's first rapscallion. There ain't nothing he can do to us we ain't seen." Today, Mr. and Mrs. Purifoy were older than they had ever been.

The boys, seeing their quarry finally come out of the bush, momentarily stopped their assault on the wing dam. Boney piped up. "Well I'll be a lowdown, dirty milk snake hidin' in the grass. Look who's finally stepped up to take their medicine. Looks like old Boney's not the only one gonna have to take his medicine anymore. Mom. Dad. Step down to the river. Meet the famdamily."

And they went to the river, arm and arm. They climbed over the sandbags and made their way down the protective berm toward the river. They walked slowly, but steadily, because this was their acreage and no square foot of it was unknown to them. But now they looked toward the river at the maples and willows along the bank and saw the scum line the flood had left way up on the trunk of the trees, the high water mark. They saw driftwood and cornstalks up in the branches where they didn't belong, and they saw a toilet seat hanging from one of the low limbs like some decoration. A flock of red-winged blackbirds passed overhead casting its shadow, but then the sun was bright again and shone brightly on the green grass. Mr. and Mrs. Purifoy walked on the soft green grass, stepping around beer cans, until they approached the river and stood in front of the wing dam and the group of half-naked boys.

Boney was the master of ceremonies. "Lane, Johnny, Peabody. This here's Mr. and Mrs. Milktoast. Say, 'How do you do' boys, and say, 'How do you do' Mr. and Mrs. Milktoast."

"How do you do."

"Don't say our real names," the tallest one said, obviously nervous about what was coming to pass.

"Shut up, Lane. That's not your real name. You don't have a proper name. Those aren't your real names, are they boys?" Boney was standing between his group of friends and the two adults.

"No, those are nicknames," the tall one said. The boys were all shirtless and wearing cutoffs. They were standing in the shade of the river trees. The sun cutting through the trees left bright, leaf-like scars on their bodies. Mr. Purifoy could see that they were probably just high school boys. They were stalk-thin with hairless, sunken chests and fragile arms. They all bore tattoos in different places though, and ponytails. This gave them an air of meanness and unpredictability. There was a shorter, blond one in front with a cruel-looking hook protruding from his shirtsleeve. He had on a black hat with white lettering that spelled, *Good guys wear white hats*.

Mrs. Purifoy was the first to speak up. From her spot on the bank, she and her husband looked down at the boys. She gripped her husband's sweaty hand, then surprised herself with how calmly she spoke. "What is it you want from us, Nathan?"

"Shut up Lila. You know what I want. These boys are mercenaries. They just want to have a little fun with something that ain't theirn. But I got a special mission. I wanna get back something that was mine that you took away. You and Milktoast here took away something that belonged to me. I want you to put it back in my hands." Boney raised up his hands and held them out. They were grotesquely large, pruned from the river water and cut with sunlight.

"She goes her own way, Nathan," Mr. Purifoy said. "You know that."

"Nathan? Who's that? Now I got a name to you old man?" Boney bent and palmed a skull-sized rock. He held it up to examine. "Now I'm not Long Hair or Hippie Freak or Phoney Boney? Now I got a real name like you, Frank, and you, Lila? Now I'm as good as you?" Boney stepped up from the edge of the wing dam onto even ground with Mr. and Mrs. Purifoy. They could see he was drunk because his thin, purple knees were unsteady below his jagged cutoffs. He was drunk, and crazy too. His skull cap hid his eyes as he spoke. "Well that suits me fine Ma and Pa because your daughter done been rode hard and hung up wet, and now she ain't no good to nobody but old Boney. Now that I'm as good as you all, you can just deliver her back to me, and I'll take good care of her just like she likes. Give her back to me." He looked up then, and a wide blade of sunlight cut his eyes.

Mrs. Purifoy could see that Boney was crazy. But she could see something more than madness in his minnow eyes, ringed in black. She could see pain there. Pain like she knew. She saw Boney framed with the river behind him and the woods beyond that, and it was as if she knew him. She saw that perhaps this boy was just another victim and not the villain she had thought him to be.

"Why you poor boy," Mrs. Purifoy said with sincerity. "Don't you know that we lost her too? We lost our little girl even before you. You're just like us Nathan, too witless and slow to keep up. You've been stuck here in this backwater too long, and now you're trying to splash about to get yourself noticed. It won't work. We've got a room in our house, Nathan, and it's called regret. We live in it."

Mrs. Purifoy let go of her husband's hand and pointed a dirty finger at Boney. "You've been passed by, Nathan, just like us. Get in your little pirate ship and head down river. You're not anchored here. There is an old wooden bridge downstream a ways where you can take out, and another after that."

For a while it appeared that Boney was taking these words to heart. He turned and looked down river, craned his neck to see around the bend. But he was not so easily cowed. He brandished the big rock in the air, hefting it easily, then he cannonballed it into the deep water where it made a thunderous splash. "You can't talk to Boney that way," he said. "You turned your daughter against me. You ruined everything for me, and now it's time something of you was ruined too."

Boney's friends stepped off the wing dam and stood beside him. Mr. Purifoy stepped in front of his wife. He held his arms out in a scarecrow pose. He tried to look intimidating as he stared at the young boys. He had a reputation as a head-knocker. Maybe he could get mileage from that. He glowered with his meanest face. But he became dizzy then, and wobbled, leaning back lightly into his wife's bosom. There was a whirring of insects. He lost track of himself, and for a moment he was back in his garden. All his daughters were with him there, all young together, wearing their Sunday dresses. He was teaching them to plant seed, how to use your finger to space the seeds so they would have their own room to grow. But his Carmen was scattering the pretty pink seed about recklessly. Soon there might be wild corn growing in amongst the pumpkin vines.

A fish hawk screamed high above, and then Mr. Purifoy's head cleared. He was looking again at the boys. The sunlight had softened, and the blades of light on their bodies had turned to fingers. He raised his own dirty finger in disbelief, for it appeared to him suddenly that the long-haired boys had no ears. He tipped into the arms of his wife.

Boney was in supreme command then. "Let's up to the house, shall we?" he said, draping a long arm uphill. "We're gonna have a looksee what's livin' in that special room of yourn."

Mrs. Purifoy did as she was told. She practically had to drag her dazed husband back up the berm. She thought this might be the end, and she was envious that Mr. Purifoy was off in some other place.

Boney ordered the adults indoors. Then he turned his cronies loose, and they ran amuck in the backyard. Mr. and Mrs. Purifoy watched from behind the sliding glass patio door as the boys ascended the berm, rose over it. They watched as the boys pulled up the birdfeeder and swung it wildly around until they smashed the birdbath. Boney watched too, a gaunt pirate atop the hill, as the boys moved on to Mrs. Purifoy's flowers, starting with her bright orange poppies. They yanked them up one by one, swinging the large and hairy plants around by their pretty heads, striking each other with the dirty roots.

Yet as she watched, Mrs. Purifoy herself was not surprised. She felt that she had known this was coming all along, was almost grateful that it was finally here. Soon, the worst of the flooding would be over, and the high, dirty water will have floated off downstream. Mr. Purifoy, on the other hand, had not yet come back to her. He was still shaking from his vision at the river, staring blankly off to some other place. "There, there," Lila said, smoothing what was left of his hair. "We'll replant the flowers, and the birds will always love us if we feed them."

But Mr. Purifoy wasn't listening. Or he couldn't hear. The earless boys had his young daughters out in the yard, ravishing and spoiling them, trampling their pinafores and dragging them by their beautiful strawberry hair. And his daughters' muffled shrieks of terror sounded almost like delight.

Home & Garden

Bluets and black flies arrive on the same bus. The same spring sun, rain and warming temperatures that bring the heaven-reflecting flower bring, in far greater numbers, the clouds of swarming, buzzing, biting flies...To admire the bluets, you must peer at them through a veil of torment.

—*The Old Farmer's Almanac,* 2011

Changing Room

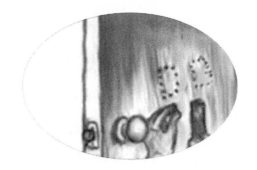

There is the cabin and the space Connie occupies in the cabin—then there is the cabin and the space his brother Dale occupies in the cabin. While the baby sleeps in the cabin, and while the family splashes on Bergamot Pond, Connie crouches in the suffocating utility room. The house back home doesn't have a utility room, but the cabin does. It's not much bigger than a closet, but the door is on the outside, whereas a closet door would be on the inside. Here in the utility room is evidence of Dale. Here Dale crouched low on the moldy green carpet remnant—had the carpet remnant been moldy then?— and, with a hammer and a nail, pounded his initials into the knotty pine of the utility room door. The door must have been closed, which means that Dale would have been closed in the utility room like Connie is closed in now, with the light bulb on. He must have smelled the same stuffy utility room smell of mildew and spilled 50:1 boat gas that Connie smells now. He must have been lonely to close himself in the utility room and pound his initials into the door. Everyone else must have been down to the fun lake splashing, else someone would have heard the pounding and put a stop to it to save the baby's sleeping.

The idea that Dale could have been lonely, like Connie is lonely, is dizzying. Dale in the pictures and in Connie's memories is always grinning. But Dale's initials, D.G., are pierced cleanly through the clear varnish and into the soft pine. This is clear evidence that his brother was here, alone, unhappy. *Like Connie.*

Connie finds some nails in the wooden tray of screws and washers and pipe fittings at the back of the utility room. He finds a clutter of hand-tools, as well as boat oars, a buoy, old lawnmower blades, a wooden slalom ski, a garden edger, horse shoes for pitching, but no hammer. There is a broken mirror in the back of the utility room. At one time, before Connie's time, the utility room was a changing room. The hooks holding the hand tools are clothes hooks, not tool hooks. At one time, Connie's family must have believed they needed a changing room, but it turned out over time they needed a utility room more. There are still some old changing-room decorations. Connie's mother had made curtains for the square window out of a terrycloth towel. You would need curtains in a changing room. Connie's older cousins had changed out of their bathing suits in this room. Dale too, must have taken off his wet swim suit and hung it on a hook to drip dry onto the green carpet remnant. The terrycloth curtains are red and blue in a pattern of anchors. The curtains are never open, nor the window, so the red and blue anchors on the outside are faded gray and pink, while here, on the inside, the anchors are still bright red and blue and good as new.

No one touches the curtains.

The only other decoration from the changing-room days is the knotty-pine shelf up high holding duck decoys. There are four duck decoys, two mallards and two wood ducks. Each has a chipped bill. The two mallard bills are completely chipped, while the two wood duck bills are only partly chipped. Either the bills were shot off or they broke off when someone dropped them. No one has dropped them for a long time. The decoys are just for decoration, and they sit up on the high knotty-pine shelf looking like ducks, but not quite.

Connie lugs a big pipe wrench hung from one of the clothes hooks. Maybe Dale couldn't find a hammer either. Maybe Dale made do with the big pipe wrench that never got used except to prime the pump in the pump shed once a year when Connie's family finally came back to the cabin in the spring. The pump shed. His house back home didn't have a pump shed either. The pipe wrench is heavy. Connie kneels on the carpet remnant holding the heavy wrench and some nails.

It doesn't take long, in the clammy utility room, to sweat. Connie's chest against his thigh is slippery. He wears just cutoffs, and the rest of his body is soaked in sweat. Anyone in here with the door closed would sweat. Dale would sweat.

Connie tries the nails, some big ones and some smaller ones. The biggest nail fits the hole Dale had made. So. Dale had used the biggest nail. Connie has heard talk of nails. He knows the big nails, like this one, are sixteen pennies nails. He holds the sixteen pennies nail like Dale must have held it and pounds a hole in the utility room door right below the holes Dale pounded. With the sound, he is aware of that other, bigger room, the cabin. In the cabin the baby sleeps. The screen door slamming would wake him, but Connie doesn't think this muffled pounding will. Anyway, the baby doesn't matter. It just feels good, somehow unlonely, to pound a hole.

Next to the first hole he makes more holes, envisioning the curved side of a Capital C for Connie. Each time he hits the nail with the flat back of the pipe wrench the utility room door vibrates and the nail makes a clear mark in the wood like the marks Dale made. Alone in the utility room, bent to work on his initials, Connie practically is Dale.

After Connie has finished his C, he stops to compare. When he was pounding nail holes he saw only the C, but now he can see his initial below Dale's initial. By itself, Connie's C is fine, but beneath Dale's he can see the ways his initial is inferior. For one, Connie's nail holes aren't as deep as Dale's. This means that Dale was stronger than Connie. Maybe Dale was older when he was here, lonely and sweaty in the suffocating room. Connie hadn't thought of that. He is only eleven. There is something else. Dale's nail holes are evenly spaced, while Connie's are uneven. Dale was neater than Connie, as well as stronger. He wonders now, too late, if the C of Connie should have a curve like it does when he writes it on paper. Dale made his D without a curve, so it looks like a capitalized box with two edges cut cleanly. Dale made the smarter choice. His D.G. is square and angular and even.

Connie has made just a flimsy, off-balance mess of C. He sits back, no longer crouching, his knees up. He puts his teeth to his slippery knee. Dale's sweat. He should stop now. This has been a mistake. The D.G. will never be alone on the door anymore like Dale wanted it. Now it will be ruined forever by the crooked C. The D.G. alone on the clean varnished door was Dale's brave idea. It was his original idea. Dale's original loneliness had driven him up from the fun lake to shut himself in the suffocating changing room and make his superior initials with hammer and sixteen pennies nail.

Pipe wrench! Dale would not have been so lazy to use a pipe wrench for a hammer. Connie has no idea what made Dale lonely. Connie's own loneliness isn't even original. It is just loneliness for Dale, who didn't live long enough to feel lonely for Connie.

The duck decoys, with their chipped bills, look fake. Connie may as well finish the bad job. The G will pose no problems. Connie can just copy Dale's G exactly, then he can punctuate the C.G. with deep periods and be done with it.

From somewhere, from the cabin, Connie hears the screen door slam. Someone entering the cabin from the lake didn't read the sign, written in black marker on a paper plate and taped to the screen door: Baby Asleep! Don't Slam Door! Now the baby will wake. The screen door always slams, paper plate or not. The baby always wakes. The screen door is old. It has never been changed. There were probably paper plates for each of the babies in the family. There must have been a paper plate for Connie, for when he was a baby.

Connie waits. He crouches on the green carpet remnant chewing on his sweaty arm. Dale's arm. He waits for the baby to wake.

Instead of the sound of a baby crying, Connie hears the screen door slam again. Someone leaving. Normally when the screen door slams the cabin shakes to its rafters. No baby could sleep through that. But out here in the utility room the sound is muffled. It sounds like a screen door slamming on a house next door. So. In the utility room, it is easy to believe the sleeping baby doesn't hear the screen door slam. Adults are murder when the screen door slams. The baby wakes. But maybe not this time. Maybe this time there will be time to finish.

There is the cabin and the sleeping baby, and then there is the changing room and Connie crouched beneath the quiet decoys. While Dale was in the changing room, Connie was just the stupid baby he hoped would sleep through the noise.

Marigolds

From the time I started to the time I flunked out, I rode to school on the same yellow No. 416 school bus with the same old bus driver and most of the same kids. Every day we went down the same dusty country roads, had the same conversations and judged the seasons by the same long corn fields. Year by year we grew out of the same blue jeans and inherited the same seats further back on the bus. Probably the only unique thing about our bus was that we had what everyone called our own stripper, a retarded girl who sat in the back named Marigold Bates.

Most people, when they hear the word Marigold, think of those yellow or orange flowers their mothers used to pot on the window ledge when the last of the snow was finally gone again forever. When I hear Marigold, though, I think of two things. First, I think of the giant fawn-colored Great Dane we used to have whose name was also Marigold. She didn't look like a Marigold and I don't know why my mom picked the name, but she did, and we all got used to it. We had Marigold for only about three years. I was just a kid then, and I used to ride on Marigold's back and make her take me sledding with her tail. We were great friends, I remember, until at some point she got to disliking me and started snapping. That's when Mom and Dad decided to have her put to sleep, because they didn't want her ripping my head off or anything. When it came time to kill her, I cried and everything because I didn't want her to go. I even hugged her around that big lovable neck, but all she did was growl because it was all over between us by then anyway. Dogs, I've learned, seem not to forget if you're mean to them. But in the end you can always put them to sleep with a big hypodermic needle and get a new dog, a puppy, and give it a new name which you'll get used to, eventually.

The other thing I think of when I hear the word Marigold is the retarded stripper who rode on my school bus. Probably there was a time that, when I heard the word Marigold, I envisioned those pretty flowers Mom brought back from the greenhouse in trays, and remembered their sharp, stinging odor when I buried my nose in them. And Mom, kneeling in her cutoffs, outside planting them. Sunny days with muddy hands and bright blue Wonder Grow. But now I have to try hard to get back that far. Those other Marigolds always come first to mind.

Marigold the girl was a couple years older than the high schoolers, but she rode with us on our bus because she went to a Special Ed room in our school. She rode in the back of the bus, where only the older kids were allowed to sit. She rarely said a word, Marigold, but we could always tell what kind of mood she was in just by looking at her face. Sometimes she had a smile that wouldn't go away, and other times she looked so lost and withdrawn that you couldn't imagine she could smile at all.

We all knew that the school had to provide that special room for Marigold because she was the only retarded girl in the district. Some of our parents talked about what a waste of taxpayer money that room was, especially because it came with its own teacher for Special Education. They say that when Marigold first moved to our district, she even had her own special van that came to her farmhouse and picked her up for school every day and took her to her special room. The school superintendent evidently used the excuse that the jarring, bouncing ride the bus provided disturbed Marigold's thinking. But the parents complained so much about all the extra taxes that the Shady Valley School Board eventually cut the special van out of the budget. My friend Reeves Booker, who was a country kid too and lived along the other side of the river, had a father on the school board and knew all about it. His dad voted to cut the van, Reeves said.

That girl might need special education, Reeves said, recalling his dad's argument. We all know she's looey in the cabooey. But I'll be goddamned if she needs a special chauffeur to get to school. She can sit on these bench seats the same as the rest of us kids. She might not have it upstairs, but her back end is the same as ours. Reeves pretended that his father's argument was his own, but I knew he was full of it because he used words like chauffeur and looey in the cabooey. We were only in grade school at the time. And when Reeves said, I'll be goddamned, he pretended that was his too, like he would actually be goddamned if Marigold got a special ride to school. Reeves was always doing that.

My feeling now is that they probably should have kept the van, and not because Marigold needed special shock absorbers. My feeling is that old Mr. Knutson, the superintendent, knew that too. I'll bet he was just afraid of telling those school board members what he thought their kids were capable of.

I don't think anyone had to ask Marigold to strip. The first time I think she just offered it. The older kids said she used to lower her pants whenever she felt like it, but by the time I was old enough to want to look at a naked girl, someone had to ask her. It was harmless because she never took it all off, and for years all we got was a glimpse of the creamy white flesh just inches below her pants line. A few of us would gather round her, blocking the aisle so Mrs. Purifoy couldn't see us from her rear-view mirror. Then someone, always an older kid, would say, Hey Marigold, let's see your back porch.

Marigold would get that corny-looking smile on her face and nod her head yes. Then she'd roll over on her side a little bit and pull her pants down a few inches. If someone asked her to, she'd usually pull them down a little farther, but for a long time that's all we ever saw. Mrs. Purifoy kept a pretty close eye on us. If she caught us gathering up back there she'd yell in her hoarse voice, You boys sit down and leave that girl alone.

I don't know if Mrs. Purifoy knew exactly what we were seeing back there. If she had, you'd think she would have solved the problem by seating Marigold at the front of the bus, but she never did.

It wasn't like we wanted Marigold to perform every day. She wasn't a pretty girl. She wore those thick glasses, and she was overweight and dressed in plain elastic pants and a sweatshirt. When you looked at Marigold you mostly felt sorry for her. My dad always used to say of our Marigold, God that dog is dumb. Look at her face, not a glimmer of intelligence. Marigold the girl had that kind of sorry and glazed look. Her eyes just stared blankly at you. Her hair was black and stringy and hung in the way of her pale oval face. Her cheeks drooped over the sides of her jowls like they were glued on. There were dark circles under her eyes.

Maybe it was because Marigold was so hopeless and sad that no one was ever nasty about what we did to her. Some days we'd ask her to take the pants down further, or to lift her shirt up high to her breasts, but she'd always shake her head no at a certain point, and pretty soon we'd stop badgering. We never touched her. You could even say we were kind to her. If she happened to drop her books in the schoolyard or get lost on the way to the bus, one of us would help her and point her in the right direction. We felt oddly responsible for Marigold, and she was safe on our bus.

There were plenty of things to do on the bus and Marigold was only one of them. We took for granted that we had such lively and willing game among us. You'd actually think kids would be even more perverted than we were. But we had other things to think about. There was always the on-going discussion about tractors: which was the best tractor, John Deere or International; whose dad had the biggest tractor and whose tractor was paid off. And there was always the buying and selling. Someone always had a pocket knife or a Bic lighter or a tin of tobacco they would sell you.

I have a lot of those good kinds of memories. For instance, I remember waiting for the bus in our gravel driveway. My brother Hoody and I stood in the driveway and kicked scuff marks in the gravel while we waited. We could hear the bus coming a way off down the early morning road, and we stood in our spots and kicked grooves in the gravel and didn't say a whole lot and waited for the bus to come and pick us up and take us off to school. Some days it was foggy, and we couldn't see the bus, but we could hear it stopping and starting at the houses up the road. We would peer off into the morning fog, and then the fog would part and the bus would appear suddenly, and it would be there for us, yellow and whole. When the bus doors opened, we stamped our feet up the three hollow steps to Mrs. Purifoy and her dangerous fingernails, and we smelled the comfortable, rubbery smell of our school bus and picked our separate seats. We did that for years.

There was a gradual changing of the guard on the bus, and one year Reeves and Vince and me, and the rest of the kids our age on the bus, found that we could sit pretty much wherever we wanted, even behind that yellow line on the aisle floor that we couldn't cross before. By then my brother drove his own car to school and the class after him was driving, and we were right where they used to be. Kids then only usually rode the bus till they were 15 or 16, when they could drive or when they had a friend—never a brother—who could take them. Somehow, we had become the older kids who brought most of the stuff to sell, and it was up to us to carry on the tradition of asking Marigold to take her pants down. We knew the rules from watching the older guys do it before us, and we did it right. It was mostly the younger kids who were fascinated because we had seen all that before.

Back in school they used to talk about classes of kids in order track them through the years. Everyone accepted this way of thinking, including parents, teachers and students. There would be a class of over-achieving students who were good athletes and had parents who were involved in the school. Then there would be a class full of kids who caused trouble and flunked their classes and would eventually drop or be expelled and whose parents seemed to encourage that sort of thing.

Everyone knew this. The reputation seemed to cling to a class, and if you were in a bad class in the first grade you would likely be in a bad class in the 12th. Mine was one of the good classes. Like good dogs we aimed to please. We were competitive in sports and our parents owned houses and came to school to watch our home games.

It was funny, then, that the students in my class should be the ones to change how things went with Marigold, who must have been 20 or 21 by then and who we thought would never graduate.

The change started with Vince, who was my age and lived up the road a couple of miles. For some reason, he started to get mean toward Marigold. I've tried to figure out why and have decided there is no logical reason. I just know that Vince had to get on the bus every day and look at Marigold. Maybe there was something changing in Vince that wasn't yet changing in the rest of us, and maybe that something made him angry at Marigold.

At a certain point you begin to notice the things that are wrong around you, and you begin to get angry at those things. When I was growing up, the stairs on our back porch were always rotted, and we weren't supposed to walk on them. No one used the stairs but my brother and me anyway, and we always just made the easy leap up or down without touching them. For years we did that. Then one time Hoody had a wild look in his eyes when we got off the bus, and he got angry at the porch. Why doesn't someone fix these goddamn rotten stairs, he said, and started stomping and bashing them in. Rotten chunks of wood and paint were flying all over us both as he crushed them. I remember watching him and being scared and thinking how bad the stairs looked now that they were bashed in.

Maybe it was something like that happened to Vince with Marigold. He started to call her the slut when he talked about her. He might say something like, Hey, how long's it been since we got the slut to show us her ass? Most of the rest of us didn't talk like that, but we never told Vince to shut his mouth either.

One day on the bus ride home from school Vince was harassing Marigold. She performed her old maneuver in the same unchanging way she always had, rolling on her side, sliding the pants down a ways, blushing almost, but smiling.

C'mon Marygoldy, how 'bout a little more, Vince encouraged. She obliged and pulled them down further. Just the top of her crack was showing. I was sitting there watching, amused, like I had done a hundred times before, like the others were doing and had done. Now a little more, chicken dove, Vince said, his voice soft and fake. But there was a line that she drew for herself, and she shook her head no, and it would end like it always ended, and we were all going to go back to our seats when suddenly Vince blurted, Take 'em all the way down, bitch. Let's see your stuff. C'mon, bare ass. Marigold turned red and shook her head no, and that's when Vince flipped and grabbed her elastic pants and tugged them along with her white cotton underwear all the way to the floor.

We gaped. There was a long, unbelievable whiteness that started at her waist and went down, forever down to the floor. I looked, and probably everyone else looked, to that spot where the whiteness started to see if we could see something more. But there was nothing for me to see, and all I could do was just look blindly and pretend it was all OK.

Then, from the back of the yellow No. 416 school bus, there came from Marigold an awful noise like a rusty bolt broke loose. She opened her mouth wide, and it looked like a cavern, and there were tiny rubber bands holding the backs of her braces together and they snapped and Vince was sort of half giggling when her arm shot out and busted him in the nose and blood, his blood, spurted all over the both of them.

There are few silences that compare with the silence that comes from a group of guilty boys. Mrs. Purifoy was upon us. We said nothing and just let her look at our guilty faces. What made it worse was that Marigold still had her pants down. She had regained her dumb indifference and sat there half smiling, maybe from all the excitement she was able to create. Girl, get your pants up, Mrs. Purifoy said, and helped Marigold pull them up and cover herself.

You've always been such good boys, Mr. Knutson told us, one by one, as we were forced to go into his office and tell the story. That's why I can't figure out how this happened.

But there was nothing for him to figure out. Our stories matched. We had seen to that the night before on many phone calls, and we convinced Mr. K. this was only a fluke.

She pulled her drawers down and was diddling with herself, Reeves said, sounding like his dad. We were watching her I admit, but then Vince got embarrassed and told her to pull them up and then he reached to help her and she decked him.

We even got Wendy Petrowski to collaborate. Wendy was a pretty freckled girl who was a year younger and didn't mind sticking up for us. The girls on our bus, though they didn't condone them, never objected or even seemed to pay any attention to our games with Marigold. They had their own agenda, which didn't include Marigold Bates or John Deere.

It passed. Wendy sealed it. The whole thing blew over. Marigold stayed on the bus. We stayed on the bus. Vince never got suspended. There were no calls home. The next year I could drive to school.

I could go on and on about what I thought was wrong with Marigold, but the truth is, I didn't know and nobody else knew. She was retarded and didn't talk. Maybe she could only speak some other language. She lived on a farm down the road, and her dad wasn't a very clean farmer. He had second-rate equipment and rented most of his land and didn't have much to do with anyone. Marigold came and went with us on the bus and never changed and kept sitting in her same seat and going to her special room, and we didn't really even ask questions about it.

She was just always there, just like Shady River was always there running backwards, and when the bus rolled into town, just like the broken-down Hilton Hotel was on the corner of Main Street by Loomis Gas, and Girlie Ellefson was standing around underneath of it with his long blond hair and dirty sweat pants and front lip full of snuff, standing as a symbol of the fate of all the town's underachievers. It wasn't like she just showed up one day, like a new kid, like something new to think about. Marigold was around long before any of us. She had always been there.

When a school bus is stopped you can't pass it. On a school bus there is a capacity of 65 and no standees are permitted. When a school bus gets used up, a new one comes along just like it. Same bus, same rules. From a school bus you can see that farmers plant in the spring, harvest in the fall. There are certain things you can't change and never even think about changing.

After I turned 16, I only had to ride the bus when I was grounded for drinking or staying out late with Wendy Petrowski. Marigold was still there in her old seat, and I sat as far away from her as I could and didn't look at her. At school, I was still in the college prep classes, but some of the kids from my bus were starting on the vocational track. Vince and Wendy were. Reeves was with me. Marigold was on her own special track in the special room by the Industrial Arts room where Vince was most of his time.

The rules were different in the I.A. room. Expectations were definitely lower. Kids could chew snuff and drink cokes and even go outside and smoke if they wanted to because there wasn't much promise in them. The I.A. room was where people always got caught and suspended for smoking pot or feeling each other up.

When we were seniors, Vince's younger brother Emerson was on the vocational track already, and he was only a freshman. Emerson rode the bus, and he was from a bad class, and one day he did something worse than his brother probably ever even imagined.

Did you hear what my kid brother did? Vince asked. It happened we were both on the bus that afternoon. Emerson wasn't. Vince's tone was serious, and I figured his brother was suspended again. Vince motioned me to his seat. He was in the very back seat. I was sitting over the wheel well, four seats up, where you don't get hit so much by the potholes. Marigold Bates was on the bus. I saw her sitting between us on the other side where she always sat. There were some other kids scattered around, but they seemed far apart when I walked by and put my hands on their seats.

What'd he do now? I asked, sliding next to Vince like you do on a bus. We were on gravel and the bus was bouncing. It gets bad in front of houses where cars slow down. They call that a washboard. Vince told me what Emerson did couldn't be repeated. Then he started to tell me the story. The bus was really bouncing, and it was hard to tell what Vince thought about the story he was telling because his voice kept rising up and down with the bus. For a while I watched his mouth move. I think he didn't know if what Emerson did was really bad. I think he was waiting to see how I reacted, so then maybe he could decide. He went on. I felt the pressure of having to make our decision. I stared straight ahead at all the seats in front of me. Vince was still talking. I saw the backs of everyone's heads. I saw the back of Marigold's head, black and still, even on the vibrating bus. It was even with the line you were not allowed to lower your windows below. The bus was stopped. I interrupted Vince.

When? I heard a horn.

Today, 5th hour.

Mrs. Purifoy was looking at me through the long rectangular mirror above her head like she'd done a thousand times. She honked again. I looked at Vince, whose head was tilted down now. Before I got up a noise came out of my throat. It was a small noise, but it might have sounded like a laugh. Vince looked up at me, and he had that look in his eyes like everything might be OK after all.

I walked off the bus, and I was at my house. It was springtime. The front yard was full of robins. Vince's story rang in my ears: *Emerson and a friend of his from town were learning the wood lathe in I.A.* I saw that the grooves Hoody and I used to kick in the gravel were filling in. *He and his friends made a wooden ornament out of a piece of oak. Sort of a spindle.* I walked down the driveway and saw that the buds were starting to peep out of the lilacs. The robins were chirping. I heard Shady River flow. I walked around my house, past the broken back stairs and down to the river. *They stretched a condom over it and sauced it up with hair gel and used it on Marigold Bates after they lured her into the room where they keep the extra wood scraps and the old band saw.* I sat on the grassy bank of the river and looked out over the current.

A couple of days passed, maybe a week. The story got out, but no one was ever punished. When kids heard, some laughed uneasily and some didn't say anything. Someone asked them if they used their pricks, and Emerson said, Are you crazy? I heard more about how they did it to her. They had some oatmeal cookies to get her in the room. Once they had her, they talked to her softly to make her feel relaxed, as you would to a horse or a dog, and she smiled at them. That's a good Marigold, pretty flower, take your pants down. Oh, that's it, now lie down.

I guess maybe Marigold was finally changing like the rest of us, because she didn't draw that line for herself anymore. The two boys weren't violent with her, and she didn't try to hit them. They said she smiled and giggled when they did it to her maybe because it made her feel good, and maybe she thought they were being nice to her. Sometimes it's hard to tell if people are being nice or mean, if it feels good. I have a hard time with that one still.

We used to bring our Marigold in the house when we wanted to keep her from going out of the yard when she was in heat. One winter we tried one of those electric dog collars where you shock the dog by radio control to bring her home. Marigold was so big she seemed to get a kick out of it though. I remember standing on the back porch pressing the button and Marigold wagging her tail and smiling like she did and dripping blood all over. Finally we just kept her inside during that time. It was supposed to be a punishment, but she loved it because she could lie on the carpet and see us people. When she was outside she would look in the window and only see a big fawn dog with a dark face and cropped ears.

I had only a year left, but I didn't make it. One day I just put my head down on my desk and refused to do it anymore. Something was rotting away in me that I stopped trying to prevent. It would be silly to say it was because of what happened to Marigold or for any other single thing. But for some reason I started carrying a little hip flask full of grain alcohol to school with me every day. I would sip it in the john and sit in class sauced thinking about a lot of things. I would think about the old wooden bridge down the road from my house and how the bus was too heavy for it because the timbers were starting to decay. Mrs. Purifoy would have to turn the bus around in her own driveway just before the bridge, sometimes getting stuck in the snow, then drive five miles around the block to get to the houses on the other side of the bridge. Every day she did that.

Then one year some committee decided to tear out the old wooden bridge and replace it with a concrete one that could support a school bus. And every day we crossed it. And every day Hoody and I had hot oatmeal for breakfast, and Marigold the dog would try and look in the kitchen window at us. Every day, too, Marigold the girl would sit gazing out the window of the bus, gazing at her reflection, until someone released her with a request.

Sometimes I would refill at lunch with the big bottle in the back of my truck, and the afternoons would blur together. Sometimes I thought about what happened in that room with the old band saw with the rusty, broken blade that had once taken off a boy's arm. I would get the voices confused, and sometimes it would be my friend Reeves' voice, or his father's, that was wooing Marigold. That's it. That's a good girl. See how easy? Such a good girl.

It would be other voices too, but I'll stop there. Marigold seemed less affected by the ordeal. She might have even smiled more. I noticed one day she carried a new white purse with a golden buckle. By now she was wearing makeup too, and some days she arranged her hair with plastic flowers.

Before the year was over, I was ineligible for everything that was important to me at that time. Rather than trying to fix all the things that were deteriorating around me, I decided to go far away. I've gone as far away as I can, which has never been far enough.

Acknowledgments

I owe many debts I cannot repay. I owe my parents first, Donald and Marilyn Fink, for supporting and never questioning, and for all that love. I owe my teachers, going all the way back, who saw some small thing and nurtured it: Connie Worden, Carol Davies, Roald Tweet, Lisa Dale Norton, Ellen Hunnicutt, Tom Bontly, Sheila Roberts and especially John Goulet, who showed me the way and bought me the suit; I owe all the editors, who also saw something, too many to name here, but Ronald Spatz was the first, at Alaska Quarterly Review and Bryan Tomasovich the latest at Emergency Press; I owe my friends in the craft, Christopher Grimes and dear, sweet Lupe Solis, Chad Faries, Jayson Iwen, Kristen Iversen, Phil LaMarche, Dan Libman, Molly McNett, and Cris Mazza; I owe the Silicon Valley Arts Council and the James Sanger family, for their financial support; I owe my creative and generous colleagues at San Jose State University and Beloit College; I owe my students, especially those few who asked what else I was up to, especially Lindsay Sproul and Kaitlin Stainbrook. I owe my friends and family who don't care how I write. I owe my wife, Breja, who believes in me and is not fickle. I owe you too, Iris. You'll see one day. I owe the woods and the waters, for their refuge. I owe many others, and I thank you all.

The following stories have appeared in somewhat different forms in the following publications:

"Amuck, The Great Engine" in *Alligator Juniper*; "Barnyard Billy Licks the Grass" in *The Malahat Review*; "Bergamot Weekly Enterprise" in *Alaska Quarterly Review*; "Boar Taint" in *The Pinch*; "Country Mile" in *Permafrost*; "Down Shady River" in *The Cream City Review*; "Every Trapper Knows" in *South Dakota Review*; "Farmer and Farmer's Radio" in *Hayden's Ferry Review*; "Marigolds" in *The Jabberwock Review*; "Heartshot" in *North Dakota Quarterly*; "Her Blue Rabbit" in *Beloit Fiction Journal*; "Horseface Cunningham Breaks His Maiden" in *Clackamas Literary Review*; "Shady Valley Days" in *Other Voices*; "Unlovely Night at the Wooden Nickel" in *Emergency Almanac*.

Emergency Press participates in the Green Press Initiative. The mission of the Green Press Initiative is to work with book and newspaper industry stakeholders to conserve natural resources, preserve endangered forests, reducd greenhouse gas emissions, and minimize impacts on indigenous communities.

The production of *Farmer's Almanac* was supported by the Antioch Media and Publishing Center in Seattle.

Emergency Press thanks Leah Rae Hunter, Frank Tomasovich, and Jill and Ernest Loesser for their generous support.

Recent Books from Emergency Press

Stupid Children, by Lenore Zion

This Is What We Do, by Tom Hansen

Devangelical, by Erika Rae

Gentry, by Scott Zieher

Green Girl, by Kate Zambreno

Drive Me Out of My Mind, by Chad Faries

Strata, by Ewa Chrusciel

Various Men Who Knew Us as Girls, by Cris Mazza

Super, by Aaron Dietz

Slut Lullabies, by Gina Frangello

American Junkie, by Tom Hansen

EMERGENCY PRESS
emergencypress.org
info@emergencypress.org

Chris Fink is a professor at Beloit College in Wisconsin where he teaches literature, creative writing, and journalism. He is the editor of the *Beloit Fiction Journal*.